The Movie N(
By MT]

This is a true story.

What to Expect in This Movie
Chapter One A Family is Born Page 4
Chapter Two Our Story Begins Page 13
Chapter Three Time to Go Page 36
Chapter Four The Break Down Page 46
Chapter Five On the Road Page 61
Chapter Six Unsupervised Teens Page 71
Chapter Seven The Trip to Yellowstone Page 82
Chapter Eight Back at Home Page 96
Chapter Nine Noah's Ark Page 104
Chapter Ten Childhood Memories Page 113
Chapter Eleven Yellowstone Page 120
Chapter Twelve Bible Camp Page 139
Chapter Thirteen And Then There Were Two Page 150
Chapter Fourteen Stink Finger Page 156
Chapter Fifteen A Sandstorm Page 161
Chapter Sixteen Family Values Page 170
Chapter Seventeen US Highway 1 Page 177
Chapter Eighteen Rollerskating Page 183
Chapter Nineteen Monterey Page 188
Chapter Twenty Fighting Page 195
Chapter Twenty One A Legal Guardian Page 202
Epilogue Page 209

Chapter One

A Family is Born

My Mom's Playlist:
    I Can't Help Falling in Love
    Elvis Presley
    Sherry
    Frankie Valli and the Four Seasons
    Hello Darlin'
    Conway Twitty
    Wasted Days and Wasted Nights
    Freddy Fender

THE MOVIE NEVER ENDS 5

My parents, like all of us, were from overlapping eras as they grew up. My mother and father grew up during the forties to the sixties until the time that I was born. Both my mother and my father were born in 1942.

My mother was what I would call "a good Catholic girl". She grew up in a strict Catholic family and even went to a Catholic school. I remember her telling me how mean the nuns were to her and her sister during school. My mom had one sister, and they were twins. Her father died when she was at a very young age and her mother remarried. She always complained that her stepfather was very mean to them. Their house was located in a middle-class neighborhood and was located only one block away from Churchill Downs Race Track, home of the Kentucky Derby.

I remember visiting the Churchill Downs Race Track when I was very young. I never watched horse race, but I walked around the stables looking at the horses and even petting them at times. There were also riding stables near by and I remember riding horses along the roadway.

She had never done drugs, or even drunk alcohol prior to leaving her home in Kentucky. She grew up in Louisville, Kentucky, which is located right smack dab in the middle of the Bible Belt. I remember her telling me that the worst thing she had ever done as a child was steal one of her mother's cigarettes. She stole the one cigarette from her mom's purse while her twin sister kept watch. Then she and her twin sister sneaked behind their garage to smoke the cigarette. She told me she was so scared! She also said it made her sick. This didn't stop my mother from smoking cigarettes for most of her adult life.

She told me of days in the fifties and nights when she went to watch the "submarine races". This meant she went to park and neck (make out for you young ones) in a car with a boy for some kissing and maybe more, but for my mom, never sex. Somehow, she ended up in California working as a secretary for an attorney.

My Father's Playlist
Born to Be Wild
Steppenwolf

That is really all there is for my father's playlist. I am the one putting the song there, not him. He always said he didn't like music. I don't really remember him listening to anything at all. He drove a taxi cab for over twenty years in St. Paul and Minneapolis. Even then, I don't remember him listening to music, and if I turned on the radio, he only complained. At times he would put it on a radio station that played classical music and tell me that was real music. He, of course, didn't know whether it was Beethoven or Bach. And I really think he just put it on those radio stations just to bother me.

My father was the complete opposite of my mother. They could not be any more different. My dad grew up very poor and worked picking up metal in garbage dump. His father owned a garbage company, and my dad would spend his days picking the metal out of the garbage so it could be exchanged for money. His father died of cancer when he was just sixteen. My father once told me that if his family had kept the garbage business, our family would have been rich.

As it turns out, his father, my grandfather, was an alcoholic and he lost that garbage business. My father grew up with an abusive father, which he blamed for a lot of his actions later in life. He told me that he was really the only child out of seven who got beat by his father. He figured it was because he was the oldest child in the family.

My father said that his dad would often tell everyone to get dressed up to go to dinner. Then they would all drive away in the family car, but first, my grandfather had to stop at the bar for a drink. My father says that was as far as they ever made it. His mother and their family would sit outside the bar waiting for my grandfather to return to the car drunk. Eventually, if my grandfather didn't return, my grandmother would go into the bar and make him come to the car.

My father talked a lot about buying cheap cars and getting into trouble on the West Side of St. Paul in Minnesota. He always talked about having long, black, and greasy hair that the girls loved to run their fingers through. My father bragged about how much "Brylcreem" he could put in his hair.

Brylcreem[1]

Brand of hair styling products

Brylcreem is a British brand of hair styling products for men. The first Brylcreem product was a hair cream created in 1928 by County Chemicals at the Chemico Works in Bradford Street, Birmingham, England, and is the flagship product of the brand. The cream is an emulsion of water and mineral oil stabilised with beeswax. It is notable for the high shine it provides, which spawned the name of the product, stemming from "brilliantine" and "cream".

Eventually, my father was remanded to a boys' ranch due to his illegal activities. Later in life, for my dad, it was either go to jail, or enlist in the armed forces. He chose the latter. He joined the United States Navy during the Vietnam War.

He cleaned the boilers on the Navy ship. He always talked about how it was a very hard job. The boilers were located in "the hole" which was usually in the bottom of the ship. The boilers were actually where water was brought to a boil on a ship. He hated that job and couldn't wait to leave the Navy. He told me he never really saw any action during the Vietnam War, because he was always on a ship. He ended up being stationed in California, which is where this unlikely couple met.

They met at a pool party, so the story goes. My dad was on shore leave, my mom had heard about the party through a friend at work. Apparently, my dad picked up my mom and jumped into the pool with

1. https://en.wikipedia.org/wiki/Brylcreem

her in his arms. I remember my mom telling me how handsome my dad had been back then and that he looked like Elvis.

If you look at photos of my father, it is true. He really did look like Elvis Presley. As it turns out, my mom, the "good Catholic girl and virgin" (yes, she was a virgin), got pregnant on that first night and our family was born.

Chapter Two

Our Story Begins

THE MOVIE NEVER ENDS

Playlist
 Jive Talkin'
 The Bee Gees
 Ballroom Blitz
 Sweet
 Philadelphia Freedom
 Elton John

Although I never thought that I had an especially poor childhood, or even a bad childhood, there is one thing that writing this book has taught me. It is amazing what a person can come to believe is acceptable and normal in this life.

My name is David, Davey to my fiends, I was born in 1965. I grew up during a strange overlapping period in the history of the United States of America. I was very young during the sixties, but I have very vivid memories all the way back to the age of two years old. I spent my childhood years wearing plaid or blue jean bell-bottoms and listening to Elvis and Frankie Valli, because these were the records that my mother owned at the time.

During the summer, my hair grew long, which I loved as a young child. But unfortunately, my father didn't think it was acceptable to go to your first day of school with long hippie hair. This meant that my dad promptly shaved off our heads down to nothing just in time for school to begin. I hated that. I hated going from having long hair to nothing. I remember being alone and crying about it. Long hair was cool, and short hair was for the poor kids. Luckily, my hair grew back quickly, but there was always that awkward stage in between, and during this time, my brothers and I were practically bald.

My dad was a biker and although this does not sound attractive to some (and I am sure it sounds very attractive to others, you know who you are!), it does have its perks. For one, when your dad drives up in front of the school on a Harley and leaves you off at school, or anywhere for that matter, you are instantly cool. But what could make you cooler? You were cooler if you could drive that same motorcycle. Although I never started the old Harley at that age, I was driving it by the age of ten. My dad would start it, then get us going down the road, I mean I was ten, I couldn't even touch the ground. But after that it was all me. I shifted and used the clutch (which was very hard to pull I might add) and I drove that beast down the highway a midst stares and wows of the other cars and onlookers we passed.

I even drove down the dirt road right past my friends as they played field hockey! That dirt road was not an easy road to maneuver. I call it a "dirt" road but it was more of a "sand" road. This meant you had to keep the motorcycle upright and straight. If you tilted too far one way or the other, as with any road bike with street tires, you would fall.

"If you dump this," my dad began, "you'll embarrass me. You will never drive it again."

"I won't."

"The sand is deep, there." He pointed and tapped my stomach.

He always tapped my stomach when he wanted my attention on a motorcycle. Like when a car passed us on the highway and there were kids in the car. The kids were staring and pointing at me and I saw the words "Wow" on their lips. I sped up to pass them and that is when I felt the tap. That tap on my stomach meant I was going too fast and needed to slow down.

For those of you who do not know, a 1948 Harley Panhead is a very, very cool motorcycle. And the way in which my dad painted it made it even more cool. But it is heavy. And even though I thought it was very fast, the truth of the matter is that it was not a fast motorcycle.

But right now we were riding through sand on the dirt road right through the middle of a field hockey game.

"Watch it. Watch the sand."

"I know dad, I know."

I went right through the middle of that field hockey game. I drove by and I even took my hand off the handle bar and waved. I didn't fall. I was proud.

As we entered the late seventies, things changed to disco and days of roller skating. Saturday Night Fever was all the rave. I was finally able to keep my hair how I liked it, which meant long shoulder length hair. I was very proficient at waltzing and dancing on roller skates, but I was never good at regular dancing. I spent those preteen years growing up during the seventies wearing silk shirts buttoned down to my navel and listening to music with the likes of the Bee Gees and other disco bands. American Bandstand was on the television with Dick Clark hosting the show. On the radio was the show we all waited for, Casey's Top 40. John Travolta and Sylvester Stallone were my movie star role models. It was a time of free love and self-awakening for many people, and I was no different.

I grew up in a small town called Willernie in the state of Minnesota. Although I lived in Willernie, I always told people that I lived in Mahtomedi, which was the city right next door. You see, Willernie was where the poor people lived, and although I grew up poor, I did not want to say I lived where the poor people lived. They even had a nickname for the people who lived in Willernie, they were called "Willards". But we were indeed poor. If we were in the movie "The Outsiders", me and my friends were the Greasers.

We never really took very good care our house or even the lawn in front of our house. I mean, we cut the grass, but that was about it. While other homes around us had asphalt and concrete driveways, our driveway was still dirt. The other houses were nicely landscaped and trimmed. Of course, we were lucky to even cut the grass, which made the grass even harder to cut when we did cut the overgrown mess. After cutting the long grass, the yard was covered in the long dead tops of the grass which we had cut off. I'm not really sure which was uglier, having long grass, or the mess left over after we cut it. You might think we would rake the dead grass away after cutting it, but that never happened.

We didn't realize it at the time, but we were much different than our neighbors. We were poor, and worse, we were young teenagers with little to no supervision.

But that was after this day in summer. It was after this fateful day, that the boys (my older brother George and I) were in charge of the lawn care. By using the term fateful day, I am not referring to someone's death. But something did die that day, that was for sure.

I wasn't thinking about the yard as I rode home on the school bus. I am not really sure what I was thinking about at all. All I know is that on this day, during my sixth-grade year, I was not happy as the yellow bus pulled up right in front of our house as usual. That was always convenient, the bus stop was right in front of our house through out my years as a student in Minnesota. But today I was not happy because I saw my dad's car parked in the dirt driveway.

My dad wasn't around very much because he had a business in the city. My mom and my two brothers and I lived out in the suburbs, but you could almost say it was in the "country". I say the "country" because beyond our small neighborhood there was nothing but endless fields of grass and trees and forests of pine. As a young boy, I rode my mini-bike for hours and hours in these fields and through the forests of pine trees, tossing up pine needles as I rode along.

When my dad was home, it would strike fear into my heart, and I was sure both of my brothers felt exactly the same way, although we never talked about it. That is why I was not happy when I saw my dad's car. My dad scared a lot of people. He scared us, he scared our neighbors, I am sure he scared nearly everyone.

Hell, even my friends were scared to be in my house when my dad was home. If I asked, "Hey, wanna come over?"

They would ask, "Is your dad home?"

If my answer was yes, they would not come over. Never. If my dad was there, I knew no friends would be anywhere near my home.

I mean, my father was not always mean. But it was that fear of the unknown, that fear of not knowing just when he might become angry for whatever reason and then he would just snap. Then he would decide to become violent. The sad part was that he wasn't even a alcoholic or drug abuser, he didn't have that excuse (if that is even an excuse). I mean, he smoked marijuana, but as far as I know, he never abused hard drugs. He was just mean at times, and well, as I remember it, most of the time. On top of his violent temper, he was a relatively large man with multiple tattoos to go along with the loud Harley Davidson he rode (hence scaring a lot of people). In addition, he kept a lot of mean-looking biker friends. Loud motorcycles were constantly part of the landscape in front of and behind our house. I remember waking up as a small child and stepping over bikers who were sleeping on our floor. I would tip-toe over the sleeping and passed out bikers to get to the kitchen to get some "Frankenberry" or "Count Chocula" cereal to eat. All of this made for a home that I am sure was pretty much feared, and probably hated, by other homeowners in the community.

The air brakes of the yellow school bus sounded "kapoosh" and then those same brakes squealed on the big old bus as it came to a stop. The door opened with that all too familiar sound that most of us know, "ka-clunk". I watched my brother as he got up out of the green vinyl seat to get off the bus.

"Dad's home," he said looking back at me. It was as if he was saying silently, "Come on!" with out saying anything at all.

"I saw."

I really felt like staying on the bus, and not going home. But that, of course, was not an option and would open a whole other can of worms. If you did not come straight home from school, for whatever reason, you were likely to be punished, well beaten. At least that was how it was at my house. I found that out the hard way one day when I stayed late to help a teacher clean the chalkboards. That day went like this:

"Your dad wants to see you." I could hear the uneasy tone in my mother's voice as she said this.

My dad was in the driveway standing in front of a car with the hood up. I didn't get to say anything. He was waiting and he was ready.

"I thought I told you to come straight home from school." My father was angry. I wasn't sure what to expect next, but I knew it would be bad. But maybe, just maybe, this time I could get out the words to explain what had happened. I mean, he couldn't punish me if I was cleaning chalkboards, could he?

"I did..." I was about to explain. I was about to tell him that I had cleaned chalkboards for the teacher, then I came straight home. I never got the chance to say those words to my father.

As usual, my dad would use whatever was closest when he was angry. For some reason, he had a screwdriver in his hand at the time. He must have been using it as he worked on the car. It didn't matter to him that he was holding what was essentially a deadly weapon. He swung the screwdriver towards my face, which I blocked with my forearm. I remember I had a dent in the bone of that forearm for years, even on this day as I exited the bus. I rubbed the dent on my forearm making sure it was still there, and like an old friend it was still there to remind me of the past and warning me of the future.

I always wondered what my face would have looked like had I not blocked the blow as he swung that screwdriver. Would he have stopped just before reaching my face? Or would I have had a mean-looking scar on my face for the rest of my life? Either way, I don't think it is something any child should have to contemplate.

In short, I stood up and followed my older brother, George, and we headed off the bus. He was older by one week less than a year. So for one week, we were actually the same age. I guess my dad and mom were busy back then. We walked around the back of the bus to cross the street to our house. I inhaled the exhaust as I walked by the back of the bus. I always loved the gassy smell of the exhaust. My dad was already outside on the steps, and my younger brother, Ted, who was three years younger, was standing by my father's side.

Now things had gotten stranger. Were we going somewhere? That was always awkward. Sometimes we did have fun with our dad. But there was always that chance, that awful split-second chance, that he might snap, and the violence would begin again.

One night, I heard a woman talking in our living room. I didn't get out of bed to see who it was, but it definitely was not my mom. My mother was at work, so I knew it was not her. I only remember my mom having one or two jobs during her lifetime and she never kept those jobs for very long.

The next morning I asked my mom innocently, "Mom, who was that woman talking in the living room last night?"

"I don't know. It must have been the television."

That was that. Okay, it must have been the television. Sounded okay to me. Unfortunately, that was not the end of the conversation. For just like today, my brothers and I got into a car with my dad. I was sitting in the middle with my two brothers on the sides enjoying the window view. We drove slowly and when we were out of sight of the house the car stopped. We had no idea why. Without any warning, the back of my father's hand hit my face with such force that I saw stars.

"Don't you ever tell your mother when I have someone in the house!"

He put the car in drive and we were driving as if nothing happened, except of course for my red face and tears coming out of my eyes. I assumed he was angry because of what I had said to my mother. I couldn't think of anything else I had said. So now I was wondering if we were headed down that same road. We were going for a ride and was someone about to get hit?

"I need to talk to ya guys, come here." My father motioned towards the driveway and towards his car.

All three boys walked over to the car. We turned around and leaned against it. So far I felt better, because we were not leaving so at least he was not going to punish us in the car. But we weren't out of the woods yet. So, there we were, lined up youngest to oldest. If someone were watching they would think we were lined up by height for some reason.

Thinking back, I wonder why it was that we were allowed to do this, lean on my dad's car that is. But then again, he was never too concerned about his cars.

He was, however, very concerned about his motorcycle, the 1948 Harley Davidson Panhead. It was his pride and joy for sure. He was always painting it different colors. Every winter the gas tank and fenders came off and by the following summer it would be a different color, a different scheme. The frame was chrome, as was most of the engine. This left only three things to paint, the tank and the two fenders. One year it was flames and the next year it was fancy designs and sparkles. I remember one year it was red white and blue just like the motorcycle in "Easy Rider". My mother would later tell me that she hated that movie. She said she hated it because it was this movie, "Easy Rider" with Peter Fonda and Dennis Hopper, that started my dad down his path to be a biker.

But I doubt that is true. He may have been a military man when they met, but my dad was always destine to be a biker. It was in his blood, just like it was in mine.

My mom said that when she met my father, he was a military man, he was a sailor. She had always loved a man in uniform. She thought she was marrying just that, a military man. She had no idea what he was before that. She had no idea that he was a juvenile delinquent prior to his military career. She had no idea that he would become a long haired tattooed biker. The tone of disgust was always apparent in her voice when she talked about this.

"He could have been so many things. He even got a job at Ford once (she was referring to the Ford Motor vehicle plant in St.Paul), but he quit that too." She would always talk about a life that could have been.

We stood there, the three boys, and stared at my dad. I waited for what I expected. There would be an accusation, maybe true or maybe just a misunderstanding, you never knew what to expect.

I remember when I was accused of taking my father's rubber mallet and pounding it on metal until it was pretty much useless as a rubber mallet anymore. When my father approached me, I had no idea what he was talking about. I had seen the mallet before, my dad had many tools and I had seen most of them. He had the mallet in his hands and it was pretty much destroyed. Yes, I knew the tool, but I certainly wouldn't ruin it on purpose.

"Ted saw you do it." My dad had that "I got you" tone in his voice.

"B-but I didn't..." I looked over at my little brother and my face was full of confusion.

Now my dad had his culprit and now the culprit didn't just ruin his tools on purpose, but he was a liar too. I got kicked in the butt pretty hard for that one. I found out later that my little brother Ted was the one who did it. And rather than be found out and beaten, he decided to blame me and actually say he saw me do it. I may have mistreated my little brother sometimes as a kid, and that might be why.

So I was waiting for this misunderstanding, or accusation and then the inevitable: a smack in the head, a kick in the ass, or both. Or worse, he might remove his leather belt which was studded with shiny chrome metal studs, typical biker attire. That always sucked. That belt hurt like hell and it left some pretty good marks. You really never knew what would happen, you were just assured that it would happen. I think the worst thing was when he had you by your hair and began kicking you in your butt. I always feared that would happen... again.

Flashback: My dad had me by the hair. I was maybe four years old. I felt my feet leave the ground. I wasn't sure if he was lifting me by my hair, or if my feet left the ground because he kicked me in my butt. My guess is that it was a little of both. Either way, I watched as my bottom half came up above my face while I was looking down. Let me tell ya, that is a scary feeling! I was so scared that I peed my pants. When my father saw that I had peed, he was enraged even more! His already angry voice became fiercely outraged and there it was, another swift kick as my hands tried to hold tight to his hand so my hair didn't get ripped out by the roots. I thought about covering my butt but then I figured he would just kick my hands. Besides, keeping my hair intact seem the more responsible thing to do. This is one time when it was not to your advantage to have long hair. I didn't know when this would end, but even this short period of time seemed like an eternity. Suddenly, I heard screaming and my head was being jerked from side to side, but the kicking had at least stopped.

I couldn't understand who was screaming! My ears were ringing from the fear, the pain, and who knows what else. It was all so confusing. I later learned that the screaming was coming from my Aunt Patty. I didn't realize it at first, but when my dad let go of my hair, I was able to turn around and see. My Aunt Patty was on my dad's back screaming at him and hitting him all about his head and face. My head was being jerked side to side because my Aunt Patty was trying to make my dad let go of me.

"Let him go!" She screamed. "Leave him alone!"

I was finally free after what seemed like and eternity and ran to our upstairs apartment to hide. The beating was over for now.

Later in life, my beloved Aunt Patty asked me if I remembered this. I told her I did. I remembered it vividly but with a numbing effect. None of these childhood beatings seemed to traumatize me. It just made me numb. But maybe some people would call that trauma.

But today was different. Today he actually wanted to talk to us. There was no beating... yet.

"I have to tell you guys something. You see, your mom and I are going to be getting a divorce."

He looked at us. We said nothing. I mean, what could we say? Yippee?

"You see, the thing is, I have another wife." He paused and looked at the ground, then looked at us again. "You also have two sisters, well, half-sisters."

You would think that I would not have a sense of relief at this statement. But I did. I mean, this did not ensure that we would not get a beating before he left that day (because he always left). But the odds had greatly improved. I also realized that there was more than one reason why my dad was never around. Sure, he had a business in the city, but he also had another family. I wondered if he was nicer to them than he was to his first family? Was he nicer to that family, than he was to us?

"Do you guys have anything to say to that?" He asked.

I shrugged my shoulders. My little brother just stared, I am not sure if he actually understood it all. I mean, he was nine years old at the time, so I assumed he did. My older brother, George, he just shook his head.

"Okay, I am going to talk with your mom for a while. You guys stay outside."

He turned and walked away. The sense of relief was nearly overwhelming! And staying outside was not a problem. We were always outside. Kids of my generation grew up outside, drinking from the hose and eating bologna sandwiches and potato chips as we ran. But now we weren't sure if this meant we could go to our friend's house, or if we should stay home. And none of us would dare go into that house and ask.

When we heard the bed squeaking inside, signaling that my mom and dad were having sex, we went into the back yard so we wouldn't have to hear. I figured this meant that nothing was going to change. I mean, why were they having sex if my dad was being unfaithful? Why were they having sex if they were getting a divorce? Did this mean she had forgiven him and now they were not getting a divorce?

We all three decided to stay in the yard and not leave. There was no sense in taking chances so my father could snap and once again we are getting beaten. Right now he was in the wrong, so maybe the day would be uneventful in the child beating area.

LESSONS FROM DAD: Now this one might surprise you. "Don't you ever cuss in front of me. I don't cuss, so you don't cuss."

My dad said this with such gravity that I knew there would be repercussions if I ever broke this commandment. So I never really cussed very much. I think I cuss more as an adult now than I ever have in my life!

Chapter Three

Time to Go

Play List

Rosalita
 Bruce Springsteen
 Ramblin Man
 Bob Seger
 LA Woman
 The Doors

I am not sure why I was thinking of that on that day, it was strange to think of that day on this important day in my life. Maybe it had to do with change, because my life was once again changing. Because that fateful day was five years ago, and now it was a summer day in 1982. That was five years ago! Five years is a lifetime for a seventeen year old teenager. Now, I was packing my motorcycle. Now, I was seventeen, and in my mind, I was a man. I was a man and I did not want to live in this small drunken little Minnesota town anymore.

My motorcycle was not quite as nice as my father's 1948 Harley. Mine was a 1967 Triumph Tiger 650cc, well, sort of. The engine was that of a 1967 Triumph, but it sat upon a Harley Davidson chopped frame. So it was a chopper and it was loud with no mufflers, and no rear shocks. It had a king and queen chopper seat, which was pretty cool at the time, but it really wasn't all that comfortable. It did have front shocks, but they really didn't work. The chopper had been pieced together with spare parts. All in all, it would be a very hard ride on the old Triumph. Bumpy roads and construction areas were sure to be felt in my kidneys on this trip. But I didn't care, to me it was cool and that was all that mattered to me. I didn't think about my kidneys, my back or even my butt. I had traded my Volkswagen bug for this Triumph Chopper. I was so excited when the guy said yes to the trade. I had been looking for something I deemed worthy to ride across the United States, and this bike fit the bill for me!

I strapped a small dufflebag to my king and queen seat, this dufflebag now contained everything I owned in the world. Prior to this day, I had spent the last couple weeks getting rid of all of my belongings, and I do mean everything I owned. What I didn't give away, I threw away in the trash. Then I strapped my sleeping bag to the front of the bike between the fender and the headlight. Both the sleeping bag and my dufflebag were encased in plastic bags, just in case it rained. Then I strapped my helmet to the dufflebag on the back. I had never really worn a helmet, it was not a requirement in the state of Minnesota. But we were headed across the states, and some states required that you wear a helmet. It was really a helmet for "just in case" scenarios.

The trip had been planned for months and today was the day of departure. And for some reason, I was thinking about the time when I was in sixth grade and my dad told us that he actually had two families. How strange!

I soon stopped thinking of this. I stopped because this short-haired, long-legged blonde was running up to my house. It was Rachel. She was coming to say goodbye. She was just fifteen, two years younger than me, but you would never have known it. She had blossomed and we had enjoyed love together for a short time that summer. We went to my room for a proper goodbye.

"Did you run all the way here?" I asked. Her house was at least four miles from my house.

"Yes."

"Why?"

"My mom wouldn't give me a ride, so it was the only way. And I wanted to say goodbye."

I kissed her. We were not together long, just a month or so. But our feeling were intense. The real reason her mom wouldn't give her a ride is because she knew my family. She worked in the school as a guidance counselor and my brother and I were well known, and not for good reasons.

It didn't take too much more time and we were back upstairs. I had two riding partners. Tim, was twenty-one, the eldest of us, but only in years. I was far more advanced on the facts of life and old beyond my years for a seventeen year old boy. Tim rode a stock 750 Triumph Bonneville. It was a very pretty bike compared to mine. It was a very pretty bike anyway you looked at it. If you are familiar with the movie "An Officer and a Gentleman", and you remember the motorcycle in that film, then you now know what motorcycle Tim was driving. He was packed and ready to go. Why was Tim leaving this shitty little town? Why had he agreed to my freedom plan to ride to California? I really am not sure why he had agreed. But he had agreed and actually bought the motorcycle and showed up to leave. If he hadn't, I still would have left alone.

Originally, it was his brother, Harold, who was supposed to ride with me. But a week after he got his motorcycle, he crashed and totaled the bike. We had spent that day riding, and it was his first time riding the bike. We had a great time riding our motorcycles that day and we were finally on our way home. Then a car stopped in front of me. I was riding on the right side, so I rode up on the shoulder to go around the car which was stopped and making a left turn in front of us, a very normal riding maneuver. I am not sure what happened, but somehow Harold didn't see the car in front of us. I heard the motor on his motorcycle accelerate and then I heard "Boom!" as he rear ended the vehicle which had stopped in front of us. At this point, I was next to the car I was passing and I watched as Harold sailed over the car to the street below. I know what you're thinking, he must be dead right? He must have landed and crashed his head into the pavement. He had to be dead, right?

I had always admired Harold's athletic abilities. We had both played football and even though I was bigger and a lineman, a defensive end for you football fans, Harold was far more athletic than I. He ran cross country and track and he was a line backer or defensive secondary in football. He was faster than I and he definitely understood the game of football better than I. I didn't understand football at all when I started. The coach just asked me to join the team because of my size.

So he put me at defensive end and said, "When they hike the ball, go for whoever has the ball."

So what happened? Harold actually tucked and rolled and came up on his feet. He was on his feet and walking towards me before I could even shut off my motorcycle. I was shocked and pulled my bike over and put it on its kickstand. Harold came walking over to me.

"I ain't got no fucking insurance!" This was all he said.

The crash wasn't serious, he didn't get hurt. But the motorcycle was no longer ride-able, the front forks and tire were bent into the engine. But the motorcycle accident scared the hell out of Harold and he never rode again. Somehow I ended up buying the motorcycle from him at a huge loss to Harold. I then sold it for a profit after I repaired it. Tim got wind of our plans and said "Hey, I'll go!" And now he was with me and along for the ride.

The third part of our party was Greg. Greg drove a Yamaha Maxim. A very pretty Japanese motorcycle. Of course, I always teased him for driving a Japanese motorcycle. Why had he joined us? Now that is a very good question. I mean, my family had no money and me leaving was not a huge surprise. I mean, it is a surprise when someone says they are driving their motorcycle across the states for a new life. But I didn't have a lot to lose in that small Minnesota town. But Greg, well his family was wealthy. His dad was a lawyer and he could go to any college he wanted to go to. But here he was, along for the adventure.

I did not tell my dad I was leaving. I did not tell him simply because I did not want to. And maybe because he might have stopped me. Not because he would have beat me. The days of beating were long over by that point, but the fear still lingered. But maybe he might have convinced me to stay. At age seventeen he no longer beat us, so I wasn't afraid of that.

After the divorce, I don't remember seeing much of him at all. I mean occasionally we went to his home, stayed the weekend and things like that. But I remember him telling me once, that the reason he stopped beating us was because my older brother and I had gotten so big. My older brother and I were good sized kids, and we were lifting weights as well. My older brother was pretty well known for his street fighting abilities. And although I am sure I rode that coat tail of a reputation, I also played football and was a pretty good sized kid at seventeen. At seventeen years of age I was 5'11" and 190 pounds. Strangely my father tried to discourage us from lifting weights.

LESSONS FROM DAD: Don't lift weights. Body builders make terrible lovers.

My dad later told me he stopped beating us because he was afraid that my brother and I might fight back one day and hurt him. Who knew? I mean I never for once thought that my dad was afraid of much of anything. As it turns out, I was wrong. He was afraid that his own children might retaliate for the years of abuse they had sustained. My dad was afraid of being beaten up by his own kids.

LESSONS FROM DAD: When you have kids, remember to kick them with the side of your boot, never with the toe of your boot. If you kick them with your toe, you could break their tail bone. If you kick them with the side of your foot, you can kick them as hard as you want.

Chapter Four

The Break Down

Play List
   (My Mom's)
   Half as Much
   Hank Williams
   Moody Blue
   Elvis Presley
   I'll Be Leaving Alone
   Charley Pride

I was still twelve years old on that summer day. After the news of my dad having a second family, my dad had left the home, and my mom had since been acting quite strange. My next door neighbor came over and told me that she needed to talk to me. She told me that my mom had walked into their house, laid on their couch, and started laughing hysterically. She had tears coming out of her eyes and she was kicking her feet and pounding her fists on the couch as she laughed. Then she stopped suddenly and she got up and left the home as quickly and as strangely as she had entered. She never said a word to anyone, she just came in, laid on the couch and did the crazy dance, and then she left. She left as silently as she had arrived.

As I said, my neighbor came over and told me about this. As a twelve year old kid, I was not sure what to make of that. I mean, she was my mom, but what was I supposed to do? She was the adult in our family, even though lately she was not acting that way, she was acting well, crazy. She had every reason to act strangely. Many truths come to light when something like this happens to a family. For one, we learned that my whole family: my Aunts, Uncles, cousins, even my Grandmother; they all knew about the second family my father had. We always thought that my father never wanted to stay at family gatherings because he didn't like to socialize. If it was Easter or Christmas we always went to my Aunt Patty's house for food and fun. But we never stayed long. My dad would rush us out, take us home, then leave for the city. Why?

Because he would then head to the city to pick up his other family. Then he take them to the exact SAME family gathering. EVERYONE knew! Every single one of my relatives, even my cousins whom I considered friends, knew about the second family. Not one of them ever said anything to me or my brother. Everyone knew except for us of course, we were oblivious.

Even the neighbors in our small community knew and apparently tried to tell my mom about it.

"He's seeing a blond girl here in town."

"I saw that same girl on the back of his motorcycle again."

One truth, there were always girls on the back of my dad's motorcycle. Somehow, that had become acceptable. It was accepted like he was being a nice guy and giving a ride to someone. This was of course, not the truth. He was always giving girls rides on his motorcycle and he was always cheating on my mom.

As I learned later, my mom really didn't want to hear about it. She would tell people just that. "I don't want to hear it," she would say in her never ending thick Kentucky accent.

I told my older brother about the incident at my neighbor's house and how our mom laid on their couch kicking her feet. He just shook his head. Neither of us knew what to do. My mom was definitely acting strangely. I think we were just hoping it would go away. We were hoping it was just a phase of getting a divorce and things would eventually change.

She was always talking about men. She specifically mention a man named Omar, he was from the middle east. I think it was Iran that she had mentioned. Omar had stopped by the house and he was selling children's bible story books door to door. I remember Omar stayed at our house for quite awhile. I left the house for hours that day and when I came back home, he was still there, but by then my mom and him were drinking and laughing. She had bought a few books and now she was entertaining. After he left she talked about him often and she talked about how they were going to be married.

"He is so handsome. I can't wait until he comes back." She would laugh. She was always laughing now, but even that was not a normal laugh. It was a nervous, uncomfortable laugh.

One day, during this crazy time, I decided to snoop a little bit and look through my mom's belongings. On top of her jewelry box, for all to see, was a folded piece of paper. I opened it and I started reading the note. It was her suicide note. It explained that she was sorry and that she loved her three sons, but she just did not want to live anymore. I think at this point, when I read the note, I read it like she was telling people she did not want to live. I didn't realize then that it was an "actual" suicide note.

On the final day before my mom departed for a year, we were at a garage sale. We were walking home from the beach. White Bear Lake was within walking distance of our home and we went swimming there often. My hair was white from the sun and my body was deeply tanned. I spent most of my summers like this only to lose the tan in the winter, like most Minnesotans. But once summer arrived I was tanned again. My mother told me it was because I had "Indian blood" in me. She was referring to Native American Indians, and it was true. My fathers side of the family had some Sioux Indian in it's ancestry.

As we were walking home, we saw a line of cars and realized that it was because there was a very busy garage sale up ahead. When we arrived, there were ten or so people with kids in tow and all of them were milling around checking out the sales. My mom loved garage sales. Everything in our house was from garage sales. Quite honestly, until I was about fourteen, I thought this is where clothes came from. At least it was where clothes came from in my household. Either that or clothes were hand me downs from my neighbors. New clothes were not even in my vocabulary.

There were toys everywhere and I had found a flashlight. It needed batteries, but at this point, batteries were secondary.

I walked up to my mom, "Mom, can I have this?"

There was no response, nothing. She was just staring straight ahead, at nothing. At this point, my little brother, Ted, came up on her other side. He had a little fire truck in his hand.

"Mom, can I have this?" He asked.

Now we were both on either side of her, and we were asking the same thing. It was then that I heard it.

"No." It was quiet, but firm, and you almost couldn't hear her.

"Mom?" I asked, noticing the strange quiet tone.

"Mom, Pleeeaassse!" It was Ted, whining about the fire truck on her other side as he tugged her arm.

I wasn't asking to have anything anymore. I wasn't concerned about the flashlight anymore. I even set it down on the table we were standing in front of at the time. I was wondering what she was doing, as she stared straight ahead at nothing.

"No." It was louder this time, but it still was not anything that anyone would take notice of.

"Mom." Again, I wasn't asking for anything, but I am not sure she knew this. At this point, I was again just trying to get her to do something besides stare and say no.

Ted on the other hand, was determined to get the truck that he was still holding in his hand as he now tugged on her shirt. "Mom! Why not?!" He whined, and the whining had grown louder.

"No!" My mother yelled now, but it didn't stop there. And now people were beginning to take notice. "No! No! Nooooo! No!" She was screaming. Now everyone noticed.

She started turning round and round in circle leaving the tables of garage sale items behind as she twirled and screamed "Noooooooo!"

I had no idea what to do. People were staring. They were staring at my mom and they were staring at me and my brother looking for some sort of explanation. We of course had no idea what was happening. No one could have known this would happen. One woman, who obviously knew my mom, walked up to her, well, as close as you could get to someone while they twirled and she started saying, "Lynn? Lynn, are you okay?"

But no one intervened anymore than that as she spun round and round, screaming "Nooooo!" It would have been hard to intervene with out her bumping into you as she twirled in the grass.

There was no explanation for her actions. I watched and I was thinking there was no way I could twirl around like that without falling. I would be dizzy, I would fall. And yes, I was correct. It was too much for her and my mother did fall. She fell and she rolled around in the grass screaming "Noooooo!"

Then the screaming got louder. She screamed "Aaaah! Get it off! Get it off!!! Nooooo!" She was crying now. While rolling in the grass she had rolled over a bee, and the bee had promptly stung her in the arm. She was crying and kicking her feet and rolling around in the yard. Sticks and leaves were in her hair and clothes and the tears streamed down her now dirty face.

The woman who was saying her name earlier ran to her side and stopped her from rolling. My mom cried and cried as the woman cradled my mom in her arms. She was no longer screaming but she was crying and in the muffled tears she just kept saying "No". This soon changed as well.

"Mud, I need mud," she said between the anguish of the tears and sobs. She was talking about needing mud for her bee sting.

I saw the firetruck as quickly as I had heard it. It pulled up and the air brakes sounded. I was reminded of the air brakes of the old school bus on the day my dad told us that he had another family. In this town, the fire department responded to every medical emergency. It was a small town and everything was very close so the truck arrived within minutes. As it turns out, and although I did not realize it at the time, this was indeed a medical emergency. My mom was in severe pain, but not physical pain. She was in emotional pain.

I remember my mom once told me, "Emotional pain is far more painful than physical pain." My mom was experiencing this kind of pain. My mom was in severe emotional pain. I cannot fathom what kind of pain was in her head as she spun around and lost control.

But for now "mud" was all she wanted, and as soon as the fireman knelt down beside her and put mud on her arm, she was better, she calmed down. I thought this might be the end of it. I thought she might get up and we would walk home. Of course, I was sure that my mom would now be talking about the handsome fireman who put mud on her bee sting. I imagined her talking about him and how she was going to marry him, just as she had talked about Omar.

But this was not the case, my mom would not be coming home on this hot summer day. The two guys dressed in white saw to that. They were not two guys from the insane asylum coming to pick up a crazy person, as you might have thought. But they were ambulance drivers and they were dressed in white, hence the metaphor rang true. My mom was more calm now as she continued to tell everyone about the bee that had stung her. She continued to talk about the bee and how she had been rolling in the grass even as the two nice gentlemen dressed in white escorted her into the ambulance. She also began talking about the handsome fireman who helped her and put mud on her bee sting. If it wasn't so heart breaking, it might have been funny, because now she was laughing again.

But once again, the laughing was not normal, and it was not the laughing I had heard over the past few months. This laughing had a shaking nervous ring to it, as if it might return to scream at any second. This laughing made you nervous just to hear it. This laughing let you know that nothing was okay in my mom's mind.

I would not see my mom for another year. And she would never be the same again. Never. She would never cook meatloaf or spaghetti and meatballs again. She would never clean the house again. She would never ever be the same mom again. She would return as a zombie. She would return a year later as a medicated zombie mom who I had to tell to take a bath because she smelled badly. I would cook my own meals in that home until the day I left. I would have to ask her to wash clothes, and she would reluctantly comply. She would reluctantly comply with all of my requests as I tried to make her be a normal mom again. But that would never happen. She would never be a normal mom again. She would walk around as if in a daze for the rest of her life.

My little brother and I walked home. My older brother was there and I explained to him about how my mom had gone crazy at a garage sale and the whole town watched. Someone had called my dad, and later that evening he showed up along with my Aunt Cindy. Luckily, as I had feared, my dad was not going to take care of us. That was my first thought. If my mom was gone, that left my dad to take care of us boys, and that would have been unbearable.

But again, luckily, my Aunt Cindy had agreed to take the three boys until my mom returned. I don't think anyone expected her to be institutionalized for over a year, especially my aunt. If my aunt Cindy had known she was taking us for a year, I don't think she would have agreed to the situation. I mean, taking care of three boys is not an easy task. Feeding, washing clothes, and cleaning up after those three boys for a year is a monumental task! Especially when my Aunt Cindy already had three children of her own with only two bedrooms to accommodate her own three children. Now she was going to have six kids in these two rooms. I really don't believe anyone would have agreed to take on three boys for a full year.

As it turned out, it was a full year until we would return home and my Aunt and Uncle did indeed take care of us during that time. I will forever be grateful for this huge undertaking. With out this unexpected gift of kindness, I am not really sure what would have happened to us. But they did take us in and I am sure it was one of the longest years of their lives.

I would spend my seventh grade year in a strange city, in a strange school, with unfamiliar surroundings, while my mother was institutionalized. My dad left the state on his motorcycle and was working in Denver, Colorado. My dad didn't go live with his other family. My dad didn't take care of his kids. My mom was crazy and in an institution and my dad had abandoned us to drive his motorcycle across the states. I actually didn't care about the second part. Being abandoned by a man who beat you and was never around was not a bad thing. But we did spend that year away from our childhood home and friends. It was hard enough losing your mother, even if she was acting strangely. But now everything in our life had changed. But that is another long story.

When I got home I immediately went to my mom's room and grabbed the suicide note which my mom had written. I threw it in the trash.

Chapter Five

On the Road

Playlist
>On a long and lonesome highway, east of Omaha
>You can listen to the engine moanin' out his one note song
>You can think about the woman or the girl you knew the night before
>But your thoughts will soon be wanderin' the way they always do
>When you're ridin' sixteen hours and there's nothin' there to do
>And you don't feel much like ridin', you just wish the trip was through
>Here I am
>On the road again
>There I am
>On the stage
>Here I go
>Playin' star again
>There I go
>Turn the page
>Bob Seger

For me, it felt like my whole life had been uncomfortable, and that I was always searching for that comfortable place. In the summer of 1982 I decided to find that comfort. I was a very good student. I played football and could have gone on to college. But I also had some of that bad biker blood passed on to me from my father. And I also had three hundred dollars and a motorcycle.

I decided we would ride to California, because well, what else would any red blooded American boy with a motorcycle and three hundred dollars do? And somehow I had talked two other teens into joining me. We left one hot Minnesota morning. I packed up my 1967 Triumph chopper and my friends and I headed west for the sun and fun and for good times on the beach in sunny California.

Tim and Greg started their bikes waiting for mine to start. Greg had electric start and it started and hummed. Tim's bike started on the first kick. My bike never started on the first kick. Never. But she did always, albeit eventually, start.

"Hey," it was Tim, "At least we're sober!"

I laughed, "Yes we are."

One more kick and my old Triumph thundered up. It was only 650cc but with drag pipes it sounded bigger, at least I thought so.

I motioned to Greg, "Well at least two of us are sober!" I yelled over the motor as it warmed up so it could idle.

"Dude!" Greg yelled!

Tim and Greg laughed. Tim was referring to the fact that we spent most of the summer drunk. I actually went two weeks without having even a single sober day. The last three years were heavy partying years for me and my friends.

I was referring to the fact that Greg started every morning with his one hit of marijuana to wake up. He wasn't exactly high, but he wasn't exactly sober either.

My mom stood on the steps watching us leave. My German Shepherd, Sargent, was sitting next to her. Earlier she had been playing fetch with my dog. I snapped a photo of her with my little 110mm camera as she threw the stick for him. My plan was to have Sargent flown to me as soon as I got settled. This did eventually happen, but it took a couple years. My other plan was for this little 110mm camera to capture our trip to California.

I led the way with my two unlikely comrades in tow. I had memorized the map in my head so I knew where to go until we found our first place to sleep that night. My sense of direction was horrible. If I didn't memorize the map in my head, I would have been lost in no time at all.

The plan:

Every night find a place to sleep before dark or near dark.

Take the scenic route until we arrived in Monterey where my friend Sam would have an apartment waiting for us.

A nice simple plan. I mean, I had three hundred dollars and a motorcycle, what could go wrong?

But we had one stop to make on the way out of town. We had to stop at the free clinic in Stillwater. Tim had a bit of a problem.

What was his problem? Well about 3 weeks prior, Tim was a twenty one year old virgin. But recently he had been chatting with a girl from Belgium. She was originally from Minnesota and had moved to Belgium, and now she was returning home. Tim and she had become pen pals and this had sprouted into a love affair. It was all Tim could talk about. He was obviously excited, a first love, and now he had a sure thing. The letters had insured that he would lose his virginity the first night she arrived. At twenty one years of age, this was definitely something to be excited about!

I was working when Tim came into the small convenience store to show off his new girlfriend. She was pretty, and had a very nice body, I thought to myself. I would have said that she was out of my nerdy friend's league if it wasn't for the sores. She had strange sores all over her body, her arms, and even her face. As I think back on it, it reminds me of the sores a crank addict might get because they are doing too many drugs. Of course I was only seventeen, and although I thought I knew it all, I had no knowledge of hard drug usage at that time.

My dad and Greg smoked pot so I had seen that drug used many times. But that was about the extent of my knowledge on drugs.

Their first night had come and Tim did indeed lose his virginity to the girl from Belgium. Unfortunately, he also found out what it was like to have a venereal disease the first time he had sex. He wasn't sure what to do, but I suggested the free clinic so he would not have to feel pain every time he went to the bathroom. Riding to California with a venereal disease would have been hell! And I was correct, a shot of penicillin and we were on our way!

We eventually made it to I35 and headed south. The crazy dream of a seventeen year old boy-man had now become a reality. We were free. We were riding. We were headed to California on a motorcycle and now I would live my own life. I had this weird feeling in my stomach, fear of the unknown maybe? But it was there, and I didn't care. I was doing what I said I would do. I was on the road on my motorcycle. If my friends didn't come, I still would have left, alone. But the terrible threesome had indeed come through and now we were headed west to California! We were embarking on a 2500 mile trip across the United States of America!

I will never forget that feeling of riding down the highway. I will never forget that feeling of freedom as I watched the blurry mirage of heat rise off the asphalt ahead of me. The hum of my motorcycle's engine, the wind in my hair, and the vibration below me all made the situation so surreal and yet so REAL at the same time. For this was real life. This was the beginning of a real life and anything could happen. The movie was playing in my mind, and in mind, the movie never ends.

That evening, we weren't sure where we would stop. But it was now dark, and we had to find a place to sleep for the night. We saw a huge campground sign. How much could they charge for a few motorcycles, right? It was after hours at the park and because it was dark, we settled down quickly. I watched all the lights go on in campers and tents as they heard my chopper rumble in. I put out my sleeping bag, so did Tim and Greg, and we watched as those same lights in those campers and tents went out. We all fell asleep in the grass under the stars.

The next morning, we found out that this campground charges as much for a motorcycle as it did for a car. And they already had us right where they wanted us, we had stayed the night and they wanted payment. But they wanted payment for each individual motorcycle. We tried to argue that we had only taken up one campsite, we hadn't even started a fire. But that didn't matter. We decided that this would be the last campground to stay in, if we could help it. My three hundred dollars wasn't going to last long it I had to pay to sleep every night.

We were still learning, it was the first day and the first night. We had a lot to learn that summer.

Chapter Six

Unsupervised Teens

Playlist
> I'm your Boogie Man
> KC and the Sunshine Band
> You Make Me feel Like Dancing
> Leo Sayer
> Sir Duke
> Stevie Wonder

THE MOVIE NEVER ENDS 49

When my mother returned home, all three boys went back home to our house in Willernie. But, once again, everything was about to change even more so.

The biggest change came when one day, my dad came to see us. He told us that one of us had to go live with him and his other family in the city. We had since met our stepmother and our two half sisters and had a pretty good relationship with them. It was uncomfortable at first, but eventually we all got along and spent nights playing games like R.I.S.K and Scrabble. My mom hated that. She hated that we had met the other children and accepted them. But as my father said, "It wasn't their fault". They had nothing to do with the mess which my father had created. Even though she was never normal again ,she was also never short on words about my father, who she now referred to as "That son of a bitch".

My older brother and I simply said, "Well, I am not going."

I remember when my dad told us that he wanted one of us to move, that is exactly what we said.

My brother and sounded off at exactly the same time. "Well, I am not going."

This left my younger brother Ted. He was the youngest and from what I can remember there was very little protest. Maybe it was because he heard us say it first. You know, the first ones to act get what they want? But I really think he just figured that he had no real voice or choice in the matter.

What was left in the home were two teenage boys with a mother who offered little to no supervision. My mom paid the bills with welfare checks. She could afford to do this in the summer. But with winter came a heating bill, and she could never afford to pay for that. She would go to Catholic Charities every winter to get financial aid to pay for the heating bill in our home. She always said that my dad never gave her money and I believe her. She never had cash and she paid with our food with food stamps. Although she was able to make sure that the mortgage and utilities were paid, she did little else. She spent her days in bed, unless I coaxed her out to do housework.

My dad did give me incentive to do well in school. He told me that if my report card was all A's and/or B's, that he would buy me dinner and I could choose the restaurant. For me that was a huge incentive. I do not remember eating out very much as a kid. I don't even remember having access to anything close to what I eat now. We never ate broccoli or even fresh carrots. If it was a vegetable, it came out of a can, it was never a fresh vegetable. This may have been from my mother's upbringing, or it may have been because food stamps and welfare checks just do not allow for much else.

At any rate, my dad promised me free dinners as long as I performed well in school. I always performed well in school. I always got A's and/or B's. I never received a dinner as a reward for those good grades. I lost count and even teased my father at times telling him how many dinners he owed me.

I got a job in a fancy restaurant. It was one of two fancy restaurants in the little town. I started bussing tables and my brother had a variety of jobs during those years. From what I can remember we had more money than my mother. We started drinking during those first years back home. My mom was very accommodating as we grew older and she would buy the liquor as long as we paid for her cigarettes. It was a win-win situation for us. Our house became a party house with liquor and girls a plenty.

We went through various stages. We started with cases of beer, then we graduated to hard liquor. We would start out mixing the drinks, then by the end of the night we were drinking it straight from the bottle. If you really want to get kids to drink hard liquor, just tell the name of a cool drink. I remember drinking sloe gin and orange juice because it was a "Slow Screw" and of course vodka and orange juice because it was a "Screwdriver". And at times we mixed all three for a

"Slow Screwdriver". There were many others I am sure, but drinking was a favorite past time at my house.

We spent many nights drinking and playing darts. We would play darts well into the early morning ours before finally going to sleep drunk. There were many nights in which I have little or no memory of what happened. One night we had a lot of people at our house.

The next morning I asked my friend, "Hey, where did everyone go?"

"You drove them home." That was his reply.

Apparently I had loaded ten teenagers into a car and given them all rides to their respective homes. I had no recollection at all of this happening. But I think that could describe many nights at my house as I was growing up. Again, I am sure my neighbors hated us.

If I didn't want to go to school, I simply didn't go. I would write the note to be excused the next morning and my mom would sign it. It is amazing to me how I kept A and B grades through that time.

With teen drinking came teen pranking, and we were dangerous pranksters. In the summer, we would hide and throw things at cars. We would throw eggs, tomatoes, even apples. In the fall came huge piles of leaves raked up on the side of the road. We would actually hide in these piles of leaves. We would bury ourselves in the leaves and as a car passed we would throw that night's items at the cars. The tires of the cars would screech to a halt. Sometimes they would just do that, then they would head down the road. Other times the driver actually got out of the car to try to find whoever had egged or tomatoed their car. I can't count the times a man stood yelling "You fucking kids!" while we were just feet away, hidden in a pile of leaves.

In the winter, materials were even more readily available in the form of snowballs. A few nicely placed snowballs on the windshield of a car and the unsuspecting driver would be quickly blinded and unable to see. All of this was done on slick slippery roads as well. Of course we weren't always crack shots so the snowballs usually hit other parts of the car but that awful "thud" would make anyone come to a screeching halt!

And let's not forget toilet-papering. We toilet papered trees, bushes, and even toilet-papered entire cars!

We even went through a phase where we started stealing signs. What kind of signs? Stop signs, yield signs, street signs, I mean, you weren't cool unless you had at least a couple on your bedroom wall (and I had a few). And of course it helped if you had a cool story to go along with how your obtained said road sign. We even stole some construction lights from barricade stands. I remember one night, my older brother stole a blinking yellow light from a barricade. My friends and I were watching from afar, it seemed like a pretty easy operation, we had checked it out earlier. We just needed a wrench, remove a couple of bolts, and the light was ours. What we didn't expect was that someone might be watching us, well, watching my brother as he performed the theft. As he successfully removed the light, we watched as he lifted it over his head in victory. We were, of course, drunk and laughing, and everyone thought he was done. Then we heard it.

"Hey you kids!"

We were safe, we were far away and we ran down the street. My brother, on the other hand, was now carrying a blinking yellow construction light in his hands. I actually thought he would drop it and run! No such luck. The construction barricade was actually right next to a forest. So my brother did not run down the street with the blinking light in his hands, he would have been caught for sure! He ran straight into the forest. My friends and I watched the whole thing, it was hilarious and we talked about it for years thereafter. We watched as this blinking yellow light zigged and zagged through trees and bushes and occasionally the light even jumped! We were laughing so hard, I was bent over and could barely breathe. Later, the next day, my brother had the blinking light in his bedroom!

As we got older and had access to cars, we became even worse. Now we could do drive-by eggings. The unsuspecting pedestrian didn't have a chance as we passed, soon peltering them with eggs. And let me tell you, eggs hurt when they hit you!

Or, we could take baseball bats and go out hitting mail boxes! You would hang out the passenger window with said bat in hand and "boom!", home run!

Yes, we were horrible. Thinking back now, I wish someone would have stopped us. Most people knew who the dangerous pranksters were. Most people knew it was us and that we had an adult in the home, but she wasn't all there. Hell, even the police knew who we were. I remember one evening I was sitting on my front porch with a few of my friends. On this night, we had not been up to no good. We were actually not pranking that night. A sheriff's car pulled up in front of our house and the deputy approached.

"I know it was you guys who egged that Corvette last night. Do you know how cold it got last night?"

We were all looking at him with amazement. We actually had no idea what he was talking about or even how he suspected us.

"Let me tell ya, it was below freezing last night. Do you know what egg does to paint below freezing?"

Again, we were all speechless. Finally, I said, "I don't know what you're talking about."

"SHUT UP!" He snapped! "I expect the responsible party to go to that house, apologize, and pay for the damage to that car. You get me?"

Again, we were speechless. He walked away, and as soon as he left, we started laughing. Yes, we were pranksters, but for once, we were innocent. We were innocent that night, but guilty of too many other wrong-doings. A mixture of alcohol and teenagers can never lead to anything good.

Chapter Seven

The Trip to Yellowstone

THE MOVIE NEVER ENDS

Playlist
- Mr. Roboto
- Styx
- Dirty Laundry
- Don Henley
- Rock the Casbah
- The Clash

The first stop on this trip was NOT supposed to be Yellowstone National Park. As a matter of fact, I wasn't going to go there at all because it was in a helmet law state. But as it turns out, that is exactly where we ended up. We headed south on I35 and then west on I90. I90 is actually the longest interstate highway in the United States and is approximately 3021 miles long. For me, it was the easiest route. Keep in mind, this was in the days before Google Maps and navigation. So when you are a seventeen year old boy, you tend to take the easiest route. And looking at the map, I90 was the easiest route for sure. I actually had more than just a map with me. I had a Map book.

LESSONS FROM DAD: Always carry a map book of any place you intend to stay in for any length of time.

A map book is a book that includes all of the states in the United States. It had the big map of all of the major highways in the United States. But you could also turn to the inside and there were maps of each individual state, in alphabetical order. There were also maps of most major metropolitan areas. So when I say we headed east on I90 that is correct. But at times, while I was looking at the individual state, I found some short cuts on smaller less frequented highways. I could never remember the exact route, even if I recreated the trip. I would just see a short cut and say, "Hey, let's go this way."

Making a trip like this left one with very interesting feelings. For the first few days, you think about everything, and I mean everything. Your head swims with the same thoughts over and over again. I was in eleventh grade and still had to finish high school. I would have to take care of that when I arrived in Monterey. That was a huge worry of mine and I thought about that a lot. After a week, the thinking slows down and on week two, you start to just think about the road, and really, nothing else.

So most of the time, we just rode, and, as I said, this gave you plenty of time to think. You thought about life, you thought about girls, you thought about everything. We would stop for gas, which was really dictated by my motorcycle. I didn't have a speedometer or odometer, so I had to count mile markers. But my chopper's gas tank was small, which meant we had to stop every eighty miles or so to fill up. Which actually worked out well, we could stop every hour and a half or so and stretch our legs, inspect the motorcycles, and eat or drink if needed.

On my first day of riding, I discovered two things. First, I had not tied the helmet to my motorcycle very well, or maybe the strap broke. But either way, something had happened, because it was gone. None of us saw it fall and roll away, which was strange. We all took turns leading the way as we rode down the highway, but you would think one of us would have seen the big ball shaped helmet bounce away down the highway. Hell, you would have thought I would have heard it. Then again, my chopper was pretty loud, so maybe, well, not maybe, because I never heard a thing, it just fell off. Somewhere on I35 there was a not so cool looking helmet sitting on the side of the road, scratched and maybe even broken. But the helmet was gone.

I imagined someone finding the helmet and seeing it all scratched and broken. I imagined them telling their friends how they found this helmet and it was so broken that the person who had been wearing it had to be dead! That helmet may be a legend in a small town right now! Hell maybe it even spawned tales of the haunted highway which was patrolled by the ghost of a lone biker! I had a good laugh about that. Even then I was a writer!

I didn't want to waste money on buying a helmet. I certainly wasn't going to ride back hundreds of miles trying to find it, especially since it was probably broken even if I could find it. So I made a decision to take a chance.

The only state in which I knew I would need a helmet was Wyoming. Wyoming was a helmet law state, helmets were required. We were not going to be in Wyoming very long. We were just traveling through a small corner of the state on our way to Montana. So I hoped that I would not see any police officers during this time. So far we hadn't seen very many cops at all while riding the interstate. Or if I did see any, I hoped that they would not see me. And if they did see me, maybe they would see my Minnesota license plate and cut me a break because the helmet was not required in my home state. All of these things played through my mind as we travelled a long. One of many thoughts during those first days of riding.

I also realized something else on that first day. As I was riding, I looked down and saw something very strange. On the left side of my motorcycle, a very large bolt was protruding horizontally from the bottom of the engine.

I looked down and remember thinking,"What the fuck is that?"

I pulled over at the first available stop to check it out. What was it? It was the main engine bolt holding my motorcycle's engine to the frame. The nut on one side of the bolt had actually broken off and the vibration of the tired thumping engine of the Triumph had slowly moved it out. If the bolt did indeed fall out it could have been disastrous. The engine would have dropped or shifted. The chain may break, wires may break, there were many bad scenarios going through my head.

I am sure this was my fault. Before we left Minnesota, I had taken the engine out. I must have over tightened the bolt when I reinstalled the engine. I was able to kick the big bolt in with my boot, but it left another problem. How was I going to keep it in?

LESSON FROM DAD: Duct tape has many uses. It is something you should carry with you always.

And I had remembered this important lesson as I removed the duct tape from my dufflebag. I wrapped the bolt that remained to the frame of the motorcycle over and over, as many times as room would allow. Luckily, because it was a smaller engine mounted on a larger Harley Davidson frame, there was actually a lot of room.

"That should hold it." I said confidently.

"Dude, we're riding to California!" Greg laughed as he puffed on his one hit.

"Yep." I said.

Tim was silent and just watched.

I90 runs west just before you reach the Iowa state border. We had ridden half of the State of Minnesota and turned right to travel across the bottom of the state, but still we were not in another state. I think that first one took the longest. At least it seemed like it took forever to finally get out of the state of Minnesota.

When we crossed into South Dakota it was "Fists in the Air"! It may not seem like much, but for three teenagers traveling across the states, every new state line was a huge victory. So there it was, "Fists in the Air" at every state line. We were now in the badlands of South Dakota. The scenery had changed and I was changing as well.

Officer Deed

The next set of fists was at the Wyoming state line. Wyoming was here and the landscape was amazing. Once we hit the state line Tim and Greg donned their helmets. I of course, did not, because I had none. We rode and enjoyed the sights we had never seen as we entered the mountains.

At this point, I90 does a sharp northerly turn heading north into Montana. I had made it most of the way through Wyoming without a sign of any police cars or any other issues. I guesstimated that we had roughly sixty miles until the Montana border. I was feeling rather triumphant because I had broken a law that I did not believe in. I hated wearing a helmet. I rode to feel the wind in my hair. I was feeling more and more confident as we closed in on the border of Montana. The last town was about forty miles behind us, and I could feel the relief of the Montana border knowing I had ridden in a helmet law state without wearing a helmet, and soon it would be of no concern.

Greg rode up beside me and I stuck out my tongue in defiance. He and Tim hated wearing the helmets as well. We came from a state where no one really wore them. I mean I cannot remember a time seeing a person in a helmet as I was growing up. I am sure I saw them on television in and old Elvis movie maybe, but not in real life. When you never wore one, it was a hard thing to get used to. And what kind of rebel wears a motorcycle helmet? They let me know at every stop with "Dude you suck" comments and the like. I just laughed.

This is when I heard Greg say "Fuck it!"

I watched as he rode his motorcycle ahead and removed his helmet. He quickly snapped it into the motorcycle lock on the side of his bike. And now he was indeed breaking the law, the same as me. There is a strange satisfaction in breaking the law and getting away with it, especially for teenagers. It was a bit of a thrill!

That is when we saw him. The purple Wyoming State Trooper vehicle came around the corner and the officer inside hit his lights as soon as he saw us. I was doomed. I had no helmet. Greg was for sure in trouble for removing his helmet. And Tim had larger problems. He still hadn't gotten his motorcycle license. All he had was his motorcycle permit, but he had no license. He was actually not supposed to leave the state with only a permit. He wasn't even allowed to drive at night with just a permit.

We pulled over and honestly I was not expecting a lot. I mean we were nearly to Montana, and it wasn't like I had deliberately broken the law. I had actually lost my helmet.

The name tag said Officer Deed. I will never forget his name, because he could have done a good deed that day. He didn't need to harass three teenagers from Minnesota. But for some reason Officer Deed of the Wyoming State Highway Patrol decided to teach us some sort of lesson. What did I learn? I learned that he was an asshole, nothing more.

I explained that I had lost my helmet, and that Minnesota was not a helmet law state.

"Son, you're not in Minnesota," he said flatly.

Greg explained that he had just removed his helmet because we were so close to Montana. Greg was very honest and I admired him for that. We were both very apologetic.

"Well, you shouldn't have removed the helmet. This is Wyoming," he said just as flatly as before.

And Tim showed his paper motorcycle permit (we claimed it was the temporary license until his real license arrived in the mail).

I also explained that we were so close to the Montana border that soon none of this would be an issue.

"But you are not in Montana son. You are in Wyoming." Flat.

None of this mattered to Officer Deed. None of it mattered at all. Greg received a citation for not wearing a helmet. While we were there, Officer Deed asked me to start my motorcycle. He noticed that it was extremely loud and that I had no mufflers. He promptly wrote me a ticket for loud/modified exhaust. I explained that this was not a violation in Minnesota. And... Yes you guessed it.

"You're not in Minnesota, son."

As for Tim, Officer Deed told us that Minnesota was not responding as to the validity of his license. Tim got lucky. He did not get a ticket.

Officer Deed informed us that we needed to pay our traffic tickets immediately. He informed us that he would escort us into town to the courthouse to pay our fines. He would also escort us to the motorcycle shop in that town so that I could buy a motorcycle helmet.

Officer Deed did just that. And in one day, I lost more money than I wanted or needed to, and we lost valuable time. Instead of arriving in Montana, we went backwards to the closest town in Wyoming. We could not continue forward towards Montana. I had to spend unnecessary funds all while be chaperoned by one of Wyoming's finest. What a dick!

Officer Deed followed us and made sure we paid our fines. He actually walked us into the court house to the window and told the young lady there, "These boys need to pay some fines."

Then he watched as we left the courthouse. He told me where to go to buy a helmet. The motorcycle shop that sold helmets was on the way out of town.

"And don't think you can leave the city without buying that helmet boy. I will know and you won't like how that ends." Those were his parting words.

I didn't see Officer Deed any longer. If he had followed us or if he was watching us, we couldn't see him. I almost decided to huff it out of town and not buy a helmet. I didn't want to spend more money. But that would have been stupid. I pictured myself getting another ticket, paying another fine, and wasting more valuable time. I stopped and I bought myself a nice shiny black helmet. It was definitely the nicest helmet I had ever owned.

I got to wear it until the Montana State line, then I don't think I ever wore it again.

Chapter Eight

Back at Home

Playlist
  My Love
  Lionel Ritchie
  Grease
  Frankie Valli
  Do You Really Want to Hurt Me
  Culture Club

That first year back at home was strange for everyone. I was now in eighth grade and something had happened while I was away for a year. I had grown and matured faster than any other time in my life. And from what people said, I had become quite handsome.

It was hard to tell people what happened and why we had disappeared. Before my mother's incident, we were in school with the same people we had been with since kindergarten. You knew that the next year you would see all of the same familiar faces. Then, all of a sudden, "poof", and just like that, we were gone. Then, "poof", all of a sudden we were back. I felt like everyone knew what had happened. I am sure most people knew that my mom had mental health issues. It was a small town, word travels swiftly in a small town.

When people asked what happened I just said, "We went to live with my cousins for a year."

With my new found good looks came lots of girl chasing. Lots of chasing that is, until I met Mary. Mary was a year older than me, she was in the same grade as my older brother. She was definitely one of the more popular and attractive girls in the school. At this point, my middle school was for grades six through nine. So she was the in the oldest grade in the middle school, kind of like the seniors of the high school, she was a senior of the middle school.

We fell in love, hard. I really thought that I would never be with another girl for the rest of my life. For me there was no other girl. She was in gymnastics and I played football, although neither of us were athletes. I was already wearing a leather jacket with a biker type of look. I am sure that most people thought that I was into drugs, which could not have been farther from the truth. I think this is one good effect that my father had on my life. Because he smoked pot, it represented drugs to me, and it was something that I loathed. I had no desire to inhale anything into my lungs, let alone do any other type of drug, except alcohol that is.

My dad never drank alcohol, not even beer. But marijuana was a whole different story. My dad smoke marijuana like most people smoke cigarettes. He drove a taxi cab in the cities of Minneapolis and St. Paul and was stoned for much of that time, over twenty years. I remember having a conversation with him once (when we got older of course). The gist of the conversation was that I told him that no matter what he says, his reaction time is slower when he was high on marijuana, so he was a hazard when he drove while he was high. He tried his hardest to convince me that he actually drove better while he was stoned. That was that.

LESSONS FROM DAD: If you decide to smoke pot, I want you to smoke it with me, no one else.

Back to Mary, yes we fell in love. We spent a lot of time together and we learned about many things together including being each other's first. We were both virgins before we met, and soon after we were like a couple of rabbits!

I had learned a lot in that short period of time leading up to my experience with Mary. One huge fact I had learned was that my dad was a liar. He had lied to everyone about his other family and his business in the city. In my heart I felt that Mary would never lie to me. We loved each other and nothing would change that.

Like so many young love stories, I learned that I was wrong. Mary had met one of her old boyfriends while she was at the beach. She kissed him. How did I find out? Her best friend told me. I remember when she came over to my house, I looked her right in the eyes and asked her if she had kissed another person. I told her I had heard it through the grapevine.

She looked me right in the eyes and said that it was not true. She told me that she had not kissed anyone. And I chose to believe her. I believe her until her best friend called me and told me she was lying.

"How do you know?" I asked.
"Because I was there." She said.

I was crushed. But I was not going to be in a relationship with a liar. We were together for eight months, and now it was over. I had seen what had happened to my mom. And more than this, I hated that my dad had lied to our family. Even though he was a poor father, it didn't change the fact that he lied. I broke up with Mary and she told me she was heartbroken. She tried constantly to get back together with me. She would come to my house, we would have sex, for old times sake, then she would leave. I would always tell her before and after that we were not getting back together.

I have talked to Mary now that I am older. She says she still loves me and that I was the love of her life. After high school she began working in a strip club. She says, "I was only the hostess, I never took my clothes off."

She headed down a very rough road of alcohol and drugs. To this day she says that the reason she started doing drugs was because I broke her heart. She swears that if I wouldn't have broke up with her that she would have never gotten involved with drugs.

I don't believe this statement of course. She had already smoked cigarettes and marijuana a couple of times when we were together. She knew I hated it. But even today I told her that I never would have broken up with her if she didn't kiss another boy and lie about it.

This was the beginning of a long line of distrust for me and created an inability to really commit in my life. I believe that I realized this all along through my relationships over the years. But something inside me just couldn't stop it. It was like, no matter what relationship I was in, I always had one foot outside of that relationship bucket. It is sad, but it is true.

I was never depressed or suicidal. As a matter of fact, I felt like I was happy pretty much all of the time. But that one foot in and one foot out philosophy would really define my life as I matured, unfortunately.

Between my father and a girl in my eighth grade year, I was pretty much out of honest relationships for a good part of my life.

Chapter Nine

Noah's Ark

Playlist
- Beautiful Loser
- Bob Seger
- Stray Cat Strut
- Stray Cats
- Born to Run
- Bruce Springsteen

So far, we had been sleeping in our sleeping bags, and campgrounds were out. We found it cheaper to pull into a wayside rest and sleep there, than actually going into any campgrounds. Wayside rests were frequent along the interstate. There were always signs saying "45 miles until next rest area", so we even knew how long it would be until we saw the next rest area. This also helped in the decision on whether we should stop and rest awhile or continue on. And most of all, rest areas were free. The signs all said that there was no camping and that there was no over night sleeping. But who's to say that a few tired bikers weren't just taking a nap. We saw police officers, but after Officer Deed, we had no issues with police or state troopers. There were always picnic tables to sleep on, and many areas had grills. We would round up some twigs and start a fire in the outdoor grills and soon the hot dogs were ready! We pretty much lived on hot dogs, bologna sandwiches, and peanut butter and jelly sandwiches. All of these foods were served on delicious and nutritious white bread of course. This food was cheap and filling! Except for the mosquitoes, sleeping outdoors wasn't all that bad.

But as we headed out of that small Wyoming town we saw the storm, and we all knew we were not going to get out of this one. So far, the weather had been perfect. We had not seen rain, we couldn't have asked for better luck than what we had had. But that luck was about to end. We didn't see any signs for wayside rests to stop at and that storm was coming fast! That storm was coming too fast and we needed to find a place to settle down for the night. Of course I was now cursing the name of Officer Deed for putting us in this situation.

Greg was the only one who had a tent, and it was a small two-man tent. I am not sure why they call it a two-man tent. I mean, two men can fit, but even that was a tight fit. And even with two men in it, there was no room for anything else, not backpacks, or any other equipment. But this night, we had no choice. The rain began and we saw a turn-off ahead on the highway. We pulled off and parked our bikes on the side of the road and set up the tent as fast as we could. Our gear and three good sized teenagers were quickly inside the tiny tent.

Greg lit up his one hit. I pulled out a pint of sloe gin, which we had called the purple death. I had packed it for just this kind of emergency. Greg was high as Hell and Tim and I started on our way into into sloe gin drunkenness. We laughed and laughed as the wind howled and the rain whipped at the tent. We realized that the tent was not really waterproof at all. The water seeped through the cloth sides making sure we were drenched. Although we were safe from the gale winds and whipping rain outside, we were kept uncomfortable because water was slowly dripping inside. We all joked at the weather which was consuming our tent.

We had pitched the tent on a hill with a slight incline, because it was the only place we could find. There was so much water that we could feel the water rushing under the tent and we joked that we were in Noah's Ark and we were going to float away. We laughed and Tim and I drank while Greg toked away. There was no room. We were drenched. No one could lay down, the best we could do was lean over and put our heads on the plastic bags which covered our belongings. We laughed until the storm quieted and we fell asleep.

It was dubbed "The Night of Noah's Ark". And although it was one of the most uncomfortable nights of my life, it would also be remembered as one of the best nights of my life as three friends laughed freely and fiercely as they travelled across the United States of America.

The next morning the motorcycles were still there. We had talked during the night that maybe they would wash away, or worse maybe someone would steal them. We got out of the tent and after ringing the water out of our clothing, we hung our clothes on a nearby tree. Everything was wet but the sun was quickly drying things. We made a breakfast of delicious peanut butter and jelly sandwiches.

This is how we ended up going to Yellowstone National Park. Before the unfortunate incident with officer Deed of the Wyoming

State Highway Patrol, I had no helmet. I could not consider going to the park. But now I did have a helmet. I had a nice new shiny black helmet. So there was no need to leave Wyoming and that is when we looked at the map.

"Ya know, we are very close to Yellowstone." I said.

We talked a bit and decided that we would head to see Old Faithful in Yellowstone National Park.

We stopped for gas as we headed on to the twisting turning roads leading to Yellowstone. I went to a soda machine to buy myself a pop. Interestingly enough, before I could even take out my money, a mechanic (and probably owner of the little repair shop) came up to me.

"It ain't working."

"Oh," I said.

Something about the way he said it made me uneasy. I felt like the guy just instantly did not like me. Maybe it was my long hair and bandana, leather jacket, or the loud motorcycle. I am not sure. But I said okay and after getting gas the trio headed out on to the road. As I looked back I watched a clean cut young man walk over to the machine and buy himself a pop.

"Chorus"
Well, you walk into a restaurant all strung out from the road
And you feel the eyes upon you as you're shakin' off the cold
You pretend it doesn't bother you but you just want to explode
Most times you can't hear 'em talk, other times you can
All the same old cliches, "Is it woman, is it man?"
And you always seem outnumbered so you don't dare make a stand
Oh, here I am
On the road again
There I am
On the stage, yeah
Here I go
Playin' a star again

There I go
Turn the page

The words to Bob Seger's song were sounding in my head. I felt I had just experienced mistreatment at the hands of a redneck gas station attendant. It bothered me. I told the guys about it later.

"Aw fuck man!" was Greg's reply.

Tim shook his head, "Yep."

We also noticed about this time that Tim's hands were looking pretty toasty. Greg and I were withstanding the sun pretty well, but Tim seemed to be suffering. His hands had swollen about twice their normal size and they were terribly red from the sun. I suggested we stop and buy some gloves to protect his hands. We found a small hardware store on the way, but all they had were white gardening gloves.

"Maybe the white will reflect the sun," I said.

We would make Yellowstone that day, but he needed the hand protection now. The white gardening gloves did the trick. Sure they were not too cool, but Tim didn't care. He just wanted some relief. Once we made it to the camp site in Yellowstone (there you only paid for a campsite, not for each motorcycle), we decided we would stay in Yellowstone for a week to rest up and let Tim's hands heal.

Chapter Ten

Childhood Memories

Playlist
  Sugar Pie Honey Bunch
  The Four Tops
  Wooly Bully
  Sam the Sham and the Pharoahs
  Help!
  The Beatles

I mentioned before that I have very distinct memories from when I was a very young age. I can remember incidents, both bad and good, very vividly from as early as age two.

At age four I remember giving half of a Popsicle to a girl that I liked. I found myself immediately being teased for it. My new girlfriend and I sat on a rock enjoying our Popsicles as others danced around us singing "Davey and Suzy sitting in a tree, K-I-S-S-I-N-G." I didn't care, I had a cute girlfriend.

For the first five years of my life, my family moved around a lot. We moved from California, to Minnesota, to Kentucky and finally back to Minnesota. We settled in the city of St. Paul and I remember living most of that time in a duplex apartment which was located right above my cousins. In those days, during the summer, the streets were frequently recovered with a spray of liquid tar and then gravel was spread over that. One of my cousins and I thought it would be fun to get sprayed by that liquid tar. As the truck came by we walked up and suddenly we were covered in liquid tar. I remember me and my cousin standing naked in a bath tub as my mom cleaned me and my aunt cleaned my cousin. They were so angry at us for getting in that mess! I don't know what my cousin was thinking, but we both just stood there smiling at each other as they scrubbed our bodies removing the now dried tar. We would both immediately stop smiling when our parents noticed, trying hard to hold in the giggles.

Speaking of which, we had no shower in those days. I only remember those huge cast iron bath tubs. To save water, my brother and I took our baths together. Now I am here to tell you, if you put two boys ages four and five in a bath tub, they are going to splash each other. They are going to get water on the floor. It does not matter how careful you are. It does not matter how many times they are told. It would be hard for one child to play and wash themselves in a bath tub with out splashing water on the floor. Now you have two kids in the bath tub, a mini swimming pool? Now it was just plain impossible to keep water off of the floor.

All I know is that my father did not believe this simple fact. My father believed that two small children could be in a bath tub and get NO water on the floor. The door flew open.

"I thought I told you kids not to get water on the floor!"

Back then clothes hangers were made of heavy wire. I am not sure they even make clothes hangers like that anymore. All I see today are plastic or wooden clothes hangers. And those metal clothes hangers were so handy! You could find a variety of uses for those old metal hangers. They were, of course, used to hang clothing, but they could also hang so many other things, like plants or tools. Many people kept them in their cars to open car doors for other people if they locked their keys in their cars. You could just bend the clothes hanger until it was just the way you wanted, and then you could pull up on the lock of the car door and it was open!

On that day, when my brother and I were in that bathtub, and yes, we did get water on the floor, my father found another use for those metal clothes hangers. He found that you could beat your children with them if they splash water on the floor.

When I was older, I told my father that I remembered that incident.

"You remember that? I thought you were too young to remember that. And besides, I only did that once." That was his response.

I have often wondered why my mother never intervened when were beaten. I would like to ask her, but she has since passed away. I wonder, was she beaten by her father as well? Did she think this was normal? It had certainly become normal for me. I do remember her telling me that she did not like her step-father because he was mean. So maybe she just thought it was normal.

I know my father never hit her. And I mean he NEVER hit her. He made that very clear from a very young age. In that same duplex, where I lived right above my cousins, there were other kids that lived over a fence in the yard behind us. At times we would have rock fights. Yes, you read that correctly, we would have wars where we would throw rocks at each other. My brother threw a rock and hit a girl just above her eye. I don't remember seeing the incident, probably because I was hiding while rocks were thrown, then throwing rocks of my own. But my dad got involved somehow because he was carrying the little girl who my brother had hit with a rock. What I do remember is that she was crying and she was also bleeding.

It didn't matter that it was a rock fight. It did not matter that those same kids were throwing rocks at us. It didn't matter who started it. What mattered to my father was that a boy had hit a girl. My brother received a beating, I think I can still hear him screaming to this day.

LESSONS FROM DAD: NEVER hit a woman. NEVER.

Chapter Eleven

Yellowstone

Playlist

Hotel California
    The Eagles
    Crazy Little Thing Called Love
    Queen
    Another Brick in the Wall
    Pink Floyd

The weather was perfect, it was not hot and usually about 70 degrees. And there was no more rain in sight. The mountain air was incredible and the mountains themselves were amazing. All of these things were new to three teens from Minnesota. Minnesota had a lot to offer for sure, the most popular thing being lakes, and well, more lakes. This of course made for a million or more mosquitoes in the summer. In the summer you swam in lakes. In the winter you would ice fish on those same lakes (I have never been ice fishing) or even drive snowmobiles across those frozen lakes. That was more my thing. I liked motorcycles in the summer and snowmobiles in the winter. Then of course there was always ice skating on those same lakes. But we had never seen mountains. We had never seen spouting geysers and crystal clear blue hot springs. This was all new to us.

Our campsite was simple. Of course, Greg had the only tent, but we didn't care. We slept out under the stars in our sleeping bags. One day a lady from England walked by. She was looking at my motorcycle. She was saying how much she liked it. I was pretty amazed because I definitely had the ugliest bike. I mean it was different than the rest because it was a chopper. But the gas tank and fenders were painted by yours truly with a can of spray paint, so it was definitely not a professional looking paint job. But she was from England and so was the motorcycle, so I understand her loyalty.

Greg walked up and pointed to his bike and proudly said, "That's my bike over there." He had a pretty bike and he was thinking that the woman would commend him on his motorcycle.

"Oh, the plastic?"

"Dude."

Tim and I were laughing uncontrollably. "The plastic!" I screamed.

The lady from England left and had enjoyed our little talk. For the rest of our stay in Yellowstone "The Plastic" was the punch line for everything!

That night we sat around our campfire just relaxing. Suddenly three girls were standing around us and our campfire.

One girl was from Ireland and had the most amazing accent.

"Hello boys!" She said. "May we join you?"

I like to remember her saying things like "a wee bit of time" and other things with a lovely Irish accent, but I don't really remember any catch phrases from her native country. Although, I did ask her to say "Let go of me Lucky Charms!". She obliged and we all laughed and laughed.

Of course the three boys were more than happy to have the three girls there. The pretty Irish girl sat with me. Another more quiet Irish girl sat next to Tim, while the third American girl sat next to Greg. Apparently they had chosen their mates for the evening.

We learned that they were part of a high school band and they were touring our country, the United states of America! The American girl was one of the tour guides for the traveling band. They were not supposed to be away from their group, but somehow that didn't bother them. This was their last night in Yellowstone, they were leaving for another destination in the morning. The girl who was American, was very much the hippie of their group. She was wearing bell bottoms and leather tasseled hippie vest. Greg wasn't that happy with his girl, because of the three, he felt that she was the least attractive. More so, he liked the Irish girl I was with. But hey, I didn't sit next to her, she sat next to me, right?

The hippie girl decided to leave and head back over to their campsite to check up on things and make sure that no one had noticed that the three girls had left their band group.

Greg saw this as his time to bug-out and went into his tent to sleep for the night. I saw this as my time to make my moves on the Irish girl sitting next to me. We started to kiss just as the hippie girl returned.

"Where's Greg?" She asked.

"In the tent," I said.

She didn't say anything else. She went right into the tent after Greg. I continued making out with my Irish Lass, nothing too serious, just heavy petting and kissing. I tried like hell for more, but she stopped my hands as fast as I moved them towards any prohibited areas of her body, which was pretty much everywhere.

Tim sat and talked with the other girl. He told me later that he was still worried about having a venereal disease, and that is why he didn't try anything with the other girl that was there. But I knew he was just inexperienced at making the moves on a girl. I was seventeen and had already been with a number of girls sexually. Remember I told I started in eighth grade with Mary, and let's just say, it WAS the late 70's.

Greg on the other hand was an entirely different story.

"Greg, how was your night?" I asked the next morning.

"Dude, who let her in my tent?"

"No one, she just went. What was I supposed to do, stop her?" I was a little shocked that he was even asking me this question.

"Dude, it was crazy."

"Really, how so?" I asked laughing.

"Dude, I didn't have to do anything. I mean I was sleeping. But I didn't have to do anything. I didn't take off her clothes. I didn't take off my clothes. She did everything and climbed on top!"

Tim and I were once again laughing uncontrollably. Poor Greg! Greg was staring straight ahead jokingly acting like he was violated.

We did a lot of sleeping in those first days at Yellowstone. Riding a motorcycle for days tires you out! But we also did a lot of walking. Our campsite was very close to the big lake aptly named, Yellowstone Lake. While walking one day we managed to find some fishing line hanging in the woods. We attached some bread to the hook and threw it into the water. Low and behold we caught a large trout in no time!

All three of us had fished before so cleaning and scaling was pretty easy. Back in Minnesota, Greg actually lived on White Bear Lake (like I said, he came from a wealthy family). And I grew up playing and fishing on that same lake. How to cook it became our next problem. That was when we met the man in the trailer next to us. He had been pretty nice and we had talked a few times. He had a beautiful diesel truck pulling a huge trailer which had all the amenities of home. He also had aluminum foil! We wrapped our fish in aluminum foil and threw it into the coals of our fire.

We three shared that fish, eating the hot flesh from the tin foil. I don't remember a fish ever tasting better in my whole life.

During the time that we were cooking our fish, the man from next door also brought us a few beers. God that tasted good! And he continued to stay to tell us about his life. As it turns out he claimed to be one of the first men to walk on the moon! I can't for the life of me remember his name. I would like to believe that on that summer day in the middle of Yellowstone National Park, that we did actually meet a former astronaut. He knew the names of all of the other astronauts, and he said he knew them well. Tim and I agreed that we would look him up as soon as we arrived in Monterey. I think we both forgot his name.

Whoever he was, or whatever he was, he certainly was a nice man who showed some kids from Minnesota quite a bit of kindness.

-How I met Greg

I was sixteen and it was my tenth grade year in high school. One day during free time in gym class, I was playing racquetball with another friend of mine. It was a pretty heated game, and we were playing pretty hard. All of a sudden in walks this kid, I would learn later that his name was Greg. I had seen Greg around, but I had never really talked to him. He was a new kid in school.

He had a racquet in his hand, "Hey can I play?"

"Nah man, we are in the middle of a game." I said.

"Aw c'mon man! I wanna play."

I was like, what is this guy doing? He walked into the middle of the court and wasn't taking no for an answer. I had the ball in my hand and once again told him to leave.

"Just let me play."

"Look, get out of here or I am going to hit you with the ball." I said.

"Dude let me play."

The other guy I was playing with left and at this point and I was frustrated. I wound up and hit the ball straight for Greg. I couldn't have made the shot again if I tried. I hit him square in the nuts and he crumpled up on the ground moaning.

It is at this point in my memoir that I should mention that I was not always the nicest teenager. As I reflect, I guess I had some of my father in me. It is something that I am not proud of.

I am not sure how Greg and I became friends after that. But we did indeed become friends, best friends. We drank and partied and hung out for the entire year before we embarked on our trip west to California.

-Back to the trip in Yellowstone.

We were walking along the lake, Greg, Tim and myself. I remember it was a little chilly that morning, and the water was so clear and calm. There were little to no waves. We hadn't swam in the lake, it was too cold. But I was looking across the water when I heard Greg.

"Dude, let's fight."

"What?" I said.

"I want to fight you, I think I can take you."

First of all, I was considered the toughest of us three. It was just known. I was bigger than the other two. But apparently Greg had never gotten over that shot to the balls with the racquetball. On top of that, Greg had seen me fight before. That story goes like this:

One night at a party, I got so drunk and I started fighting with a guy. What about? Who knows? I know he was two years older than me and went to the same school. I was so drunk, I really had no business fighting. The older boy ended up on top of me and his zipper scraped across my nose, my forehead, and my chin. I wasn't letting go of him because I knew he would posture up and start punching me. At least that is what I would have done had I been on top. Eventually, the other people at the party pulled us apart, and I think this guy considered it a win for him, simply because he was on top when we were pulled apart.

I remember the next day at work getting teased by and older co-worker "Davey got into a scraper!" My face was a mess. This guy had been wearing a heavy leather jacket with a very wide zipper. It scraped my nose, my chin, even my forehead pretty badly and now they were all scabbed up!

I was so mad, and I knew I could beat this guy in a fight. I talked to his girlfriend (a girl in my grade who I had known since grade school) while we were in class that next day.

"Tell your boyfriend I'm looking for him." I said.

"Davey, leave him alone, please." She said.

I was furious because people were saying I had lost the fight. There was no fight. We were pulled apart, and hey, I was drunk. I wasn't drunk the next day. If I had seen him in school that day I would have walked up to him and punched him in the face. That was my plan. Fortunately he didn't come to school that day.

Apparently the talk with his girlfriend did the trick, because he came into the convenience store which I worked at (it was a small town, everyone came into that convenience store at least once a week) to let me know that he got my message. He was followed by three other guys which I knew from school, they were part of the burn-out group. They were the kids that got notes from their parents so they could go behind the school and smoke cigarettes in the smoking area. I know, the eighties were a different time. Just a note from your parents and you could smoke right in front of any teacher right on the school grounds. Hell, you were actually smoking with teachers!

"I would've punched you in the face if I had seen you today." I said. We both knew I couldn't do anything just then because I was working. I continued stocking shelves, but had an eye out for a surprise attack, should he and his friends try anything. I acted like I wasn't worried at all.

"Well that wouldn't have been fair." He said.

It was quickly confirmed that we would meet behind the laundromat the next day after school for a fight.

The next day, I brought my older brother along to the fight, just in case my opponent had any ideas about attacking me with the burn-outs he had with him the day before. My brother was very well known as a fighter in the school. These guys wouldn't try anything with him around. Some how Greg tagged along on the event as well. It was a pretty uneventful fight for sure. He would throw a punch, I would block it and hit him square in the nose. After a few of these he fell and I walked over and kicked him in the face. I am not sure why I kicked him in the face. I think maybe it was because he was just so pompous telling everyone he was going to kick my ass. I felt bad the minute I did it. He didn't deserve a kick in the face.

Later my brother told my dad about the fight. My dad (a street fighter by nature) made a comment I will never forget.

LESSON FROM DAD: "You don't kick a man in the face, unless he is a really dirty man."

That made me feel even worse about kicking him.

Then I got on top of him, cranked my fist back and said, "Ya give?"

He conceded and the fight was over.

I saw him a few days later, it was Thanksgiving day and I was working the cash register at the convenience store. I am sure if he had any other choice he would have chosen not to come through the check out line and be helped by me. But apparently someone had sent him to the store and he had to buy the items in his basket. I rang him up and bagged the items. His face and mouth were badly swollen and he had a black eye from our fight.

"I hope you can chew okay today." I said. I meant it. I wasn't being mean. I genuinely felt bad.

He had a tear in his eye and I almost felt like he was going to cry. He picked up his bag and said, "Well you didn't have to kick me in the face." The words came out muffled like he had oatmeal in his mouth.

It was official, now I felt really bad.

"But Greg, we're friends." I said.
"Yea, but I think I can take ya."
"Okay, you can think that."

That was all I said. I didn't care if he wanted to fight. It made me sad that he would actually want to hit me. I was his friend and I wouldn't want to hit him. Again, I thought about the racquetball to the nuts. I was about to bring it up to him. We had talked about it before, but we always laughed about it. I realized that just then, as he challenged me to fight, that it was nothing to joke about. I realized that by joking about it I was still holding this power over his head and maybe that is why he wanted to fight me. And maybe he didn't even care if he was going to lose (I was very confident that he would indeed lose). Maybe it was something he just needed to get out of his system. Maybe he just needed an apology. I was about to say it. I was about to apologize, but Greg broke the silence.

"I'm leaving tomorrow."

Tim looked at me, then we both looked at Greg.

Greg continued, "Yea dude, I mean, I got college and everything to look forward to. I can't go live in California."

I was still sad from the fact that he wanted to fight me. I wasn't sure what to say. And this surprise bit of news made me forget about that all too important apology.

He looked at us, "You know what I want. I want to be a forest ranger. I want to sit in a watch tower all day with a little bud and a little honey (marijuana and a girl). That's all I want. And Boze (he called his father "Boze") is gonna foot the bill and make that possible."

I looked at Tim. "And you? You coming to California still?" I was not angry. I was simply asking. If he had said no I still would have rode my motorcycle all the way by myself. There was no animosity. They both knew my plan. As it turns out, Tim decided he was still going to California as well.

Greg never got his apology. I remember later in life trying to find him on Facebook just so I could apologize. I never found him on Facebook or anywhere else for that matter. I missed my opportunity. He deserved an apology. I hope that he is sitting in a watch tower in the middle of a forest somewhere smoking weed with his girlfriend. I truly do.

The next morning he packed up and rode back to Minnesota alone. Tim and I stayed another week in Yellowstone before finally packing up and heading west again.

Chapter Twelve

Bible Camp

Play List

Silly Love Songs
    Wings
    December 1963
    The Four Seasons
    50 Ways to leave Your Lover
    Paul Simon

Part of being poor is having access to programs that others do not have access to (unless they lie about their income that is), such as school lunches. For as long as I can remember, we had free school lunches during all of my school years. It is actually a very good program. Once a month you receive a month's worth of tickets for school lunches. Those tickets look just like a movie ticket. You take them to school, hand them to the lunch lady in the lunch line and magic! You receive a hot school lunch. Aside from the debate about how healthy the school lunches were, at least poor kids got a hot meal once a day in the school.

I guess the only problem was that my ticket was a different color than most of the tickets that the other kids carried. I remember during my first years of elementary school that didn't matter.

If someone asked, "Why is your ticket a different color?"

I simply said, "I don't know."

In the beginning, I didn't know. But as kids got older, and meaner, they did know. And they wasted no time in telling others that the other color meant that you were a poor kid and you got free meals. The only good thing I had going for me was that I was a bigger kid, and I was a tough kid. I don't remember anyone ever making fun of me for getting free lunches.

I remember a girl said something once, "Oh, those are for the poor kids." She said answering the question of another kid who had inquired about the ticket color.

They both looked at me, then they looked away.

Another great program was the Union Gospel Mission Bible Camp. How much was bible camp? It cost one dollar! Well, it cost one dollar for poor kids. One dollar! Then me and my older brother were gone for two weeks. My mother and father were free of the two older kids for two whole weeks!

Everything was provided for us for that one dollar. The bus picked us up and shuttled us to a camp far far away in Wisconsin. The camp was located on the banks of the St. Croix River. We could swim, canoe, and float on inner tubes. All of the meals were provided. All of the entertainment was provided. The only thing you needed was some pocket change in case you wanted to buy some candy from the snack shop. Otherwise everything was taken care of.

At this point we lived out in the suburbs and many of the kids going to the camp were inner city youth. We learned a lot during those two weeks. Inner city kids can teach you a lot, and kids from a biker family could teach them a lot. Of course there were the girls. My first experience with the bible camp girls was when I got on the bus and saw a girl in short shorts with her legs spread. She wasn't wearing panties and a little bit more than her pubic hair was hanging out of her shorts. She did not seem to mind, it must have been that "free love" attitude. Yes, I was learning a lot from inner city kids. My dad actually got on the bus with us the first time. He was quick to point out the girl.

"That girl's beaver is hanging out." He said to me and my brother.

But during my last stay at that camp I learned about one thing in particular. The first trip to the bible camp was memorable but the second trip was unforgettable. It was during this trip that I met Nevel, one of the camp counselors. Nevel had a special way of talking about God and during this time, with Nevel's help, I learned the true meaning of God and the bible. I was wowed by the stories of goodness and lessons learned form the good book. Yes, with Nevel's help, I became a born again Christian!

I was amazed how I had never seen this light before. Bible camp provided plenty of outdoor activities, but every morning and every night we went to church. It was unlike any church I had ever seen before.

"I am the resurrection, and the light, He who believes in me shall live a new life!"

"Father Abraham, had many sons. Many sons had father Abraham. I am one of them, and so are you."

The people sang and laughed! I sang at the top of my lungs. We danced and even put on plays acting out scenes from the bible. It was very moving.

They were also very strict at bible camp. In elementary school, the teachers had permission to spank us with a paddle. The Principal at my elementary school, Mr. Martindale, had a huge wooden paddle to spank students. I luckily never felt the sting of that paddle. And if you were paddled at school, Mr. Martindale would call your parents and let them know that you had misbehaved that day AND that he had to paddle you! Then you got into more trouble when you got home. Today's parents would sue a school Principal for spanking a kid in today's society. Back then it was normal.

At bible camp, they didn't have paddles for spanking. But they did have canoe paddles and I believe those paddles hurt a lot more than Mr. Martindale's school paddle. They warned us over and over not to tip the canoes. But what fun is that? We loved tipping the canoes and swimming with the canoe upside down. It was hilarious.

The camp counselors did not find this hilarious. They had warned us over and over again and they did not believe us when we said that it was a mistake. And they were correct, it was not a mistake. We were preteen kids playing around and not listening or following rules that we had agreed to follow. And this was not the first time we had tipped the canoes.

There were six of us. We had tipped two canoes. It was me and my brother and four other kids. What do the counselors do when you break rules over and over again? They ask you to bend over and touch your toes, that is what they do. They ask you to bend over and touch your toes right out in front of everyone. I suppose they had to make sure it was out in the open, I mean that canoe paddle was pretty big and you needed room to swing. And if any other campers happen to be walking by while you were being punished and wanted to watch, they could do just that. I don't remember how many kids were watching us that day, but it seemed like more than hundred, maybe even the whole damn camp.

One by one we did just what was asked of us. I think in those days, saying "no" to a punishment was not an option. We bent over and touched our toes in front of an ever growing crowd of laughing campers. One by one the counselor would wind up and "whack"! One by one we stood as that paddle hit our rear ends and we grabbed our butts dancing away in pain. We laughed a bit, and so did the crowd. But it hurt! One thing that made it hurt even more was that our shorts were still wet! This made that "whack" sound even louder. Needless to say, we stopped tipping canoes on that day.

But I came home that day from camp with a new attitude. I was a born again Christian! I was going to tell everyone about this light that I had seen at summer camp. I couldn't understand how I had gone my whole life without this information! And how did others live a life in sin? I felt lighter, happier, and I had a mission to tell the world what I had learned.

Who was the first person I got to talk to when I returned home? Who was I going to proudly state my newly found beliefs to? I got to talk to my father.

LESSONS FROM DAD: " You realize that the bible is just a book, don't you? It was written by a man just like me or you. No one knows if it is true or not. No one really knows who wrote it. The fact is that most of it was written hundreds of years after the incidents happened. And you know the game right? If I tell you a story, then you tell someone else, and it goes round and round the room. Well you know that when it gets back to you, it is an entirely different story. The bible is just like that. It is just like Star Wars."

My born again Christian phase ended as quickly as it had started. I was no longer a born again Christian. But it was worse than that. I was crushed and I felt betrayed by the church. I mean, how could they preach all of this goodness and leave out the important fact that the book that they were preaching from was just that, a book. They really had no idea who wrote the book that they believed in and yet they conveyed it as truth? Honestly if they had started my education with that simple sentence, things would have been different.

If they had said, "We really have no idea who actually wrote this book. We like to believe that is is the word of the almighty God. And if you choose to believe so as well, then you can live this path of righteousness."

But they didn't say that. I felt that they had left out a very important piece of information and I was angry. I wished I could talk to Nevel and ask him why he had omitted this incredibly valuable piece of information. Then I realized that it was because they did not want you to know this information. If people knew this, if there was doubt, they could lose followers. And if they lost followers, they would lose money, and no one wanted that!

I accepted that this book had good things to say. I and accepted that I was a good person for following the rules in this book. But honestly, I thought that any normal person should know enough to live by these rules. I felt any normal person should have enough common sense to know these things (I know, I was young). But I decided that I did not need religion to tell me this. I could be a good person with out being a Catholic.

I would spend a large portion of my life searching for religion. I wasn't a fanatic about it. But I read a lot and learned about other religions as well. I look at things from a very common sense point of view. But there is no real common sense in religion. But still I searched and studied and learned a lot trying to find the "light" of religion. But that is another story.

Chapter Thirteen

And Then There Were Two

THE MOVIE NEVER ENDS

Playlist
    My Sharona
    The Knack
    Hot Child in the City
    Nick Gilder
    Miss You
    The Rolling Stones

I have to admit I was a bit sad that Greg had returned to Minnesota. I was happy that Tim had stayed along for the ride into the vast unknown. Riding was actually easier now. Before this, there was always an odd man out while riding with three motorcycles. Two motorcycles rode side by side and this left one motorcycle riding alone. We all took turns riding alone. It always seemed to even out, so there was never any problem. Also, in the eighties, the speed limit was 55 MPH so going faster than the other bikes was never an issue. Tim and Greg's motorcycles were much faster than my old Triumph, even if I thought is was a cooler motorcycle.

In the eighties, motorcycles rode side by side. It wasn't until later that motorcycles rode in a staggered formation. That is how I grew up, no helmets, motorcycles side by side, and bikers everywhere.

We stayed on Highway I90 for a good long time crossing all of Montana and into Idaho. This was my first time seeing such vast expanses of land. I remember watching in awe as antelopes bounded effortlessly as if they were floating on air following our motorcycles. Towards the end of Montana came the Rocky mountains!

Words cannot describe what it is like to travel through the Rocky Mountains in the United States of America. If you have never seen them, you really need to go. And you need to drive to really experience it. And if you want the true experience, ride a motorcycle. There is a huge difference between a car and a motorcycle when you are sight seeing and traveling. A car is enclosed and smothering to me. On a motorcycle you see so much more. You smell the air and feel the wind as you sit high and see the mountainous cliffs you could so easily fall down. The switch overs were breath taking. One minute you were high above looking down at tiny cars on the highway below you. A short while later you were down where those cars were and working your way back up the winding mountain road to the next mountain. It was incredible.

We pulled over in a large sandy area to rest, and honestly, I just wanted to talk to Tim about the huge expanse of mountains we had just experienced. Also, I was a bit hungry and a peanut butter and jelly sounded pretty good right about then. We were tired and dirty and I couldn't remember our last bath. We sat on some huge boulders lining the highway, and then I heard it.

"Do you hear that?" I said.

"Hear what?" Tim answered.

"That.." I pointed towards the forest between us and the previous switch over.

"The wind?" Tim said.

"I don't think that is wind."

I walked over and started climbing down the rocks. It wasn't long and I saw the roaring water below. "It's a stream!" I yelled back to Tim. "Come on! Bring some soap! And some shorts for us!"

I had one thing in mind as I saw the stream. We hadn't bathed since we left Yellowstone National Park days ago. On top of that, my clothes were filthy! I was going to kill two birds with one stone. I wanted to wash the filth and dirt off of my body, and clean my blue jeans and shirt at the same time.

The water was run off from the melting snow above and it was freezing! But I didn't care. I jumped in and scrubbed my naked body clean. Then I took that same bar of soap and scrubbed my jeans, underwear and shirt. The water was amazing and refreshing. After bathing I don't remember my hair ever feeling softer. I loved the freedom and the cleanliness of that cool mountain stream!

Chapter Fourteen

Stink Finger

Playlist
  Do ya Think I'm Sexy
  Rod Stewart
  Blinded by the Light
  Manfred Mann's Earth Band
  Stayin' Alive
  The Bee Gees

My father spoke very openly about sex. My whole family spoke openly about sex. Most of the time it was in the form of jokes, but the subject of sex was always there, always.

When I was younger we had a lot of sleep overs. Most of the time people slept over at my house, at least when my father was not at home. I remember when I was eleven years of age, my friend and I were lying in bed talking. My friend asked me how far I had gotten with a girl.

"Third base." I said proudly.

"Wow." That was my friends response.

The next response was unexpected and from my older brother. "I'm telling dad!"

He had been listening silently outside my room. And he wasn't joking. He was going to tell my dad. And the next time we were together, he did just that.

It just so happens that the next time was a time when all three of us were riding in the car. It was me and my two brothers in the back seat of the car. As soon as he said it I was scared. I felt like my walls had come crashing down and I fully expected my father to send a back fist into the back seat and hit me in the side of the head. I fully expected the wrath of my father at any instant.

"Davey got to third base." My brother stated triumphantly. I could hear it in his voice. My brother was happy that I was going to get into trouble.

"What?" My dad asked.

"Davey got to third base," my brother said again.

"What? You're kidding me?" There was no anger in his voice. He was actually laughing. "Davey, you got the stink finger?" He laughed harder. "Wow, I didn't think you guys were already doing that."

My brother sank back into his seat. I think he was actually disappointed that his plan was backfiring. I could actually see his triumphant face turning sour right next to me. I also think that he was mad that he was a year older than me and yet I had gone further with a girl than he had. I sat there in bewilderment. My father was actually proud of me for it.

" You know what I do?"

I was speechless. So was my brother.

"After I play with her pussy a little but, I pull my finger up like this." He turned his head as he was driving and his middle finger was right by his nose. "I put it right under her nose and say, smell this!"

He laughed. I smiled nervously. This was a new experience. My father and I had found common ground. That common ground was sex with women and I felt lifted in stature a bit as we drove down that road.

Chapter Fifteen

A Sandstorm

THE MOVIE NEVER ENDS

Playlist
    LA Woman
    The Doors
    Games without Frontiers
    Peter Gabriel
    Mr. Blue Sky
    Electric Light Orchestra

We sadly left the Rocky Mountains and headed out across Oregon, both of us were anxious to make it to the coast. We had never seen the ocean and we were both excited to see it.

Oregon was windy and so sandy. We travelled west as the sand kicked up and began whipping our faces. The bandana I had worn around my neck was now around my nose with glasses covering my eyes. I only had dark sunglasses with me. In retrospect, I wish I had brought a pair of clear glasses for night riding. As the sand continued to pick up, it became even harder to see. The wind and sand whipped and tore at any exposed skin. We rode our bikes slowly which caused another problem. The traffic behind us began to back up and cars began passing us and honking their horns. As they did pass us, they caused the wind and sand to whip at us even more.

We were in a construction area and pulling over was impossible. My hands gripped the handlebars as I felt the wind try to push my motorcycle off of the road. The cars were one thing, the semi trucks were another more dangerous problem. When they passed you you felt as though your motorcycle were being lifted off of the road and you might just take flight (and then fall) at any moment! We couldn't see, we were stopping traffic, and between the cars and trucks and wind, we felt like we would crash at any moment.

Like a Godsend it appeared, "Rest area ahead". I was so relieved! By the time we reached the wayside rest, the wind had picked up even more and even when we stopped you could not see very far as we unpacked our bags. Normally we would have went to a set of picnic tables to sleep. But we could not see anything, no tables, no eating areas, nothing. It was not yet night, but the sky was dark making visibility next to zero. All we could see was the bathroom light inside a small concrete building and that is where we headed.

In most rest areas, the bathrooms were pretty clean. Unfortunately, the bathrooms in this rest area were not clean. We didn't care. The whipping sand hurt and it was even hard to breathe. We sat in a corner of that dirty bathroom and fell asleep with our heads on our dufflebags. The squeaky door opened and closed all night letting the sand flow in as truckers came and went after using the bathroom.

LESSON FROM DAD: My father always wore yellow glasses and I remember him telling me that those yellow glasses were better than clear glasses at night. And during the day he said the yellow glasses made even the cloudiest of days seem bright. Always carry night riding glasses.

When we woke the next morning, the storm was gone and the sun was shining and it was as if it never happened. If it wasn't for the evidence of the sand around our motorcycle tires and in our engines you might have thought it was a dream. But it wasn't a dream, so we cleaned the sand off the best we could. Then we let the wind do the rest as we struck out on the highway again.

More from Bob Seger:
    On a long and lonesome highway, east of Omaha
    You can listen to the engine moanin' out his one note song
    You can think about the woman or the girl you knew the night before
    But your thoughts will soon be wanderin' the way they always do
    When you're ridin' sixteen hours and there's nothin' there to do
    And you don't feel much like ridin', you just wish the trip was through

Here I am

On the road again
There I am
On the stage
Here I go
Playin' star again
There I go
Turn the page

Now I had Tim singing the song too. As we travelled farther west I realized that there was a lot more sand in Oregon than I had ever dreamed of. But the biggest thrill of Oregon was when we finally reached the ocean. I kept waiting for it, but when I looked ahead, all I saw was pine trees that seemed to last forever and ever. I started wondering when we would ever reach the Atlantic Ocean. According to the mile markers, we should have seen it, but all I could see were the pine trees that stretched on and on forever!

I rounded a bend and suddenly we were there! The rows and rows of never ending pine trees were not rows and rows of pine trees. Where the trees ended the ocean picked up and because they were close to the same color, it just looked as if the pine trees never ended! And now that ocean went on and on forever into the horizon.

I grew up in Minnesota, the land of ten thousand lakes. I had been around water all of my life. But on every lake I could see the other side of the shore. I could always look across and see the banks along the other side of the lake, the trees, the beaches, I could see everything. For some reason, this had not crossed my mind and I quickly realized how incredibly large this world was. The ocean went on forever. I couldn't see anything on the other side. I knew this before I got there, but until you see it for the first time, it never really sinks in.

I pulled over as soon as I could and Tim followed. We screamed and hollered and followed a steep path down the cliffs out onto the sand below. My boots were on but I didn't care. I ran into the surf and splashed the water into my face. There was another thing I wasn't used to, salt water. I grew up around fresh water lakes. Hell, you could drink the water in which we bathed in the mountains. This salt water stung as it cleansed. It was new, but I loved it just the same.

We headed south on Highway 1 trying to find a place to sleep for the night. We followed a dirt road and found a nice area to park in. The sand was deep and I had to find some tree branches to put under my kickstand to hold the motorcycle up. This is why I said there was more sand here than I realized. We were fast asleep in the comfort of our sleeping bags as we lie in the comfort of the soft sand. We were both suddenly awoken by the noise.

Apparently everyone knew about these sand dunes and as it turns out, this exact spot was where the people came to party and ride their dune buggies, three-wheelers/ATV's, and dirt bikes! One minute we were enjoying the silence, the next minute it was as if the wild characters in a Mad Max movie were all around us! The crazy mutants were driving their machines all around us. Luckily, no one bothered us. They were just there to ride and drink and whatever else they were all doing. We were strangers in a strange place and we feared maybe they might try to throw us out and make us move, or worse. But none of that happened. Once they realized where we were parked, they steered clear of the area but continued to ride pretty much until the break of day. Needless to say, we got a late start the next day. The noise of the machines and people pretty much kept us awake all night.

Chapter Sixteen

Family Values

Playlist

Celebration
    Kool and the Gang
    Eye of the Tiger
    Survivor
    Jack and Diane
    John Mellencamp

Even though my father was extremely violent with us, we still acted like kids. It is strange to me that kids will continue to be kids even in situations when they are abused. Such as, like any other young child, if you are in a store, you will inevitably ask, "Can I get something?"

Even though we knew it could trigger my father, we still took the chance. And the fact that we were in a public place, a store or anywhere else for that reason, we knew that this would not stop him from beating or striking us. It had happened before and we knew it would happen again.

When I was young, there was a store called Zayre Shoppers' City. We loved that store. More importantly, we loved the toy section of that store. Yes, for us, Zayre Shoppers' City was like going to Toys R Us when I was a kid. I think my mom may have even worked there at one point in my life. But for reference it was more like going to Target or K-mart, but with a bigger toy section.

On this particular day, my dad had three boys in tow. This would be one of the few times I remember being with my dad alone, although I am sure there were more. But we were walking and we walked passed the toy section.

I think I said it first, "Can I get something?"

I expected a "no", but that is not what happened. "Sure", he said. "Get whatever you want."

Both of my brothers chimed in, "And me?"

"Sure", he said, "get whatever you want, but just one thing."

We all picked plastic trucks and cars of one kind or another. I can't remember exactly what we chose, but I believe we all had some kind of plastic vehicle in our happy hands. And we had all picked large plastic cars, about as large as we could carry. But unfortunately, now we could not find my father.

We looked around and he was no where to be seen. We decided that maybe he went to the front of the store and he was waiting for us at the cash register area.

We never made it to the cash register area. We saw my dad standing right next to the main doors at the front of the store. My dad saw us and waved us to come to him. As we approached the doors he politely opened the door so we could leave.

"But dad..." I wanted to say we we needed to pay. I wanted to tell him that we were forgetting something. But we were not forgetting anything. My dad was on one of his scams.

"Ssshh, just keep walking." He said quietly.

And so we did, we kept walking and left the store with our shiny new toys in hand.

I often wondered what he would have done if someone had stopped us. In those days there was no security. Maybe they were too busy to notice and my dad took advantage of it? What would he have said?

Would he have said, "What are you kids doing with those toys?" and blamed it on us?

It doesn't matter now, because no one did stop us and we went to the car with our toys.

I also realized later that my dad had more than just a legitimate business and a family in the city. He also sold drugs in the city (I am assuming he sold them from his business). This enabled us to have some pretty cool toys growing up. We always had bicycles, mini bikes, and even a three-wheeler. Were they part of payment on for drugs? Were they stolen and part of payment for drugs? No one will ever know, but you can guess that many of the toys we had were in fact stolen. At least my mother said so. My first and most beloved mini bike was a little Honda Z50. You had to shift gears, but there was no clutch. I rode that little mini bike for years!

One house down from my house was a dirt road, and that dirt road led to a field full of paths and forests. For some reason I wasn't worried about getting caught by police in the fields and forests. It was private property so it would take a complaint to get the local sheriff involved. That would never happened.

But once I reached the road, I either had to push my mini bike, or I could ride it very slowly and act like I was pushing it along with my legs. On that particular day, when I was at the paved road and just one house away from my house, that was when I saw the sheriff's vehicle. Keep in mind, I was only about six or seven, so this was before our bad boy days which were coming in the all too near future. But he stopped and talked to me. I was walking the mini bike, so he just warned me that I could not drive the mini bike on the pavement.

I let him know that I was aware of this and shortly afterwards he was on his way and I pushed my mini bike the short distance home.

But I often wonder what would have happened had that sheriff's deputy decided to run the serial number on my little mini bike. Was it stolen? Would I have gone to juvenile hall?

LESSON FROM DAD: It is okay to steal from "The Man". But never steal from your friends.

Chapter Seventeen

US Highway 1

Playlist

New Kid in Town
    The Eagles
    Sweet Dreams
    The Eurythmics
    I Love Rock "n" Roll
    Joan Jett and the Blackhearts

If you are a biker, I highly recommend traveling US highway 1 on the west coast of the United States. Tim and I started in Oregon and headed South. Words cannot describe the experience on a motorcycle. The winding roads and cliff side views are amazing. The small towns lining the way are beyond charming. One could ride up and down that highway forever and see different things every time they rode.

In California, we even got to ride through Half Moon Bay, the scene of that famous Hitchcock movie, "The Birds". Traveling through Big Sur, the Redwoods, and even Carmel is something everyone should experience.

Somewhere along that Big Sur area we decided to look for a place to sleep for the night. We tried to find a more secluded place because the night before had been so windy that it was hard to sleep. It was so windy in fact, that at one point, the logs from our campfire blew over rolling across the sand and some even landed on top of my sleeping blanket! Now I had burn holes in my sleeping blanket!

We found a turn off along the highway with a small embankment lining the outside of the parking area. We decided that camping on the other side of that embankment would be a perfect place to rest for the night. No one could see us and there would be no wind. It was perfect!

We had no tent, so set up was easy. We gathered some brush and wood to start our normal campfire for the evening. It was just beginning to get dark when we heard the sirens. There were a lot of sirens and they were getting closer. We heard them on the highway outside, but could not see them over the embankment. We were expecting the sirens to pass as they headed to what ever emergency they were headed to.

Little did we know that WE were the emergency! Suddenly five firemen with a huge fire hose were a top the embankment staring at us. I think we were as shocked as they were. Here we are enjoying our campfire and these guys act like they are headed to a forest fire covering acres and acres of land.

The firemen were actually very nice. Apparently it was the dry season in Big Sur and campfires were prohibited. Who knew?

In addition, the fireman informed us that the Chief of the fire department lived just over the hill where we had set up our camp site (can you guess who called the fire department on us?). And apparently, the judge who handled cases such as this lived right next to the fire Chief! We were young, but we could do the math. If we were cited and/or even arrested, these two residents would not have appreciated that we were having a fire so close to their house.

Luckily there were no citations or arrests on that evening. They watched as we put out the small campfire and covered it in sand. They added a couple buckets of water just to make sure. We slept there that night, but there was no fire.

Carmel was amazing! If you have ever been to Carmel California you would know that there are no poor people in that city. The shopping area is comprised of cute little gift shops and restaurants. I am sure that two dirty bikers and my loud chopper were not a welcomed sight, but I didn't care. We headed straight down to the beach to check out the sights!

We walked along the tide pools seeing starfish, sea life and even an octopus clinging to the side of one of the tide pools. In Minnesota there was fish, but here there was life! And it was colorful beautiful life that I had only seen in movies!

Chapter Eighteen

Rollerskating

Playlist
- Jessie's Girl
- Rick Springfield
- Escape or The Pina Colada Song
- Rupert Holmes
- Kiss You All Over
- Exile

I started roller skating when I was very young. It was very a popular activity and we always went skating on Saturdays from 1 to 5 o'clock. I learned a lot during those Saturdays.

First, I learned how to skate. Then, I learned how to waltz on roller skates. Waltzing came in very handy, because once you knew how to waltz, all the girls wanted you to teach them how to waltz as well.

It was one thing to skate during a couples dance and be able to say you had a girl and you were a couple. But most people skated with both of the skaters facing forward and then they just held hands. If one of them knew how to skate backwards, then they could face each other and even kiss on roller skates. Although, if the skating rink guards saw you kissing they might just blow their whistle at you if you kissed too long.

So there was holding hands for the beginners, of course you were still better than those that had no one to skate with. Then came facing each other as one of you skated backwards. But if you were really cool, you could waltz! There were three types of waltzing. There was the basic waltz. Then you graduated to the circle waltz. And then there was the prettiest of all, shadow waltzing. I could do all three.

There were other activities as well. There was the conga trio. The conga trio was where three people followed each other and you kicked your foot in time with the beat of the music. "Down on the Corner" by Creedence Clearwater revival was always one of those songs.

And there was the Hokey Pokey, Limbo, 4 corners and so many other activities. They packed a lot into four hours on a Saturday. Of course, they saved the best for last, the couples only skate, so that couples could say a proper goodbye.

Rollerskating was all the rage and seemed like it was everywhere. Movie stars even roller skated on television! Farrah faucet, Brooke Shields, I even remember seeing Burt Reynolds in roller skates! I also remember having a poster of Cher on my bedroom wall wearing short shorts as she roller skated.

As you grew older and if the the waltzing and couples activities and dances bored you, you could always go into the back corner of the skating rink and make out. This really wasn't permitted, but with a couple of jackets thrown over you (because you were cold of course, nudge nudge) you could hide a make out session pretty well.

As we got older we graduated to Friday nights and going to the skating rink drunk. We were out to meet girls and cause problems. That didn't last long and soon most of us were banned from the skating rink. That didn't matter, there were skating rinks in other cities and all were within driving distance. We started frequenting numerous skating rinks in nearby cities, of course alcohol was always part of the equation.

Chapter Nineteen

Monterey

Playlist
  Monterey
  Eric Burden and the Animals
  What a Fool Believes
  The Doobie Brothers
  Heartache Tonight
  The Eagles

We made Monterey and quickly called my friend Sam. Unfortunately, we found Sam to be quite a disappointment. The first night we arrived we stayed in the barracks at Fort Ord in Monterey. We could only stay one night and then we had to find another place to stay. I was quickly running out of money, so something had to happen fast.

Fort Ord was a horrible place. It would be the last place you would choose to make a first impression of what the United States Army was like. The barracks was filthy, they had beer machines in the hallways (just like a soda machine, but you could buy cheap beer), and the "soldiers" were more like drunken street thugs than soldiers.

I learned later that the rate of rape and murder rates on the army base was astronomical compared to a normal city. I was happy to leave even if it meant we had to camp outside again. Although, it was nice to get a hot shower for the first time in what felt like ages! But it was even nicer to leave that army base.

We left Fort Ord and searched for a place to call home until we figured out what to do next. First, we found a place to park our motorcycles next to a Holiday Inn on the beach in Monterey. We found the dunes surrounding the hotel to be comfortable enough and slept there. The dunes also were like small hills with little valleys to sleep in. No one could really see you unless they walked right up on top of you.

But first things first, I knew I had to get a job and I had to get a job fast. The first week we were there I did just that. I found a job working in a little restaurant called "Joanie's too" (apparently named after the owner's wife).

The good thing about this place was that I got a portion of the tips every night, so cash in my pocket was great! I also got free meals, which I would bring back to the beach at night to share with Tim, because he had, of course, run out of money as well.

This was not how I expected things to be in California. Instead of having a nice apartment waiting for us in Monterey, and only having to worry about finding a job, I had to find a job so I could get an apartment! We had no where to live, but for me, going back home just was not an option. I didn't want to go back and say I failed. Sam said he would have extra money with in the month, but we learned quickly that Sam was not to be trusted.

If it rained outside we slept under a nearby overpass. Otherwise the beach was our home. I washed up every morning in a nearby Chevron gas station. For two months, that was where I washed myself and brushed my teeth on a daily basis. I am so happy the gas station attendants never stopped me. As a matter of fact, they never said anything. Maybe that was because I left the bathroom cleaner than when I arrived every time I finished bathing. It took two months, but I was eventually able to save enough money so that we could get an apartment. But we still had to live on the beach for two months before this could happen.

Tim wasn't able to find work during this time, and honestly, it may have been a good thing. Our motorcycles were chained to a street sign which was with in throwing distance from where we were sleeping near the Holiday Inn. But while I was working, Tim kept an eye on things.

I will never forget one night, while I was working, they were serving barbecue ribs. This restaurant was known for its "all you can eat" specials. So on this night, it was all you can eat barbecue ribs! As I was leaving, I asked the cook for two beers. He knew that I was bringing food to my friend every night, and on this night I begged and pleaded for a couple beers simply because they would go so good with the ribs. I added that Tim would be so happy when I showed up with beer and ribs. He objected at first because I was only seventeen. But eventually, he agreed, and when I got back to the beach, I presented Tim with barbecue ribs and a beer. It may have been our best meal while we were living on the beach.

The apartment we found was more of a studio apartment than anything else. It had a bathroom, a kitchen, and a living room (or in our case, our bedroom). Although I was happy to finally have an apartment,

I found myself missing being outdoors. We had been on the road and sleeping on the beach for about four months now, and I really missed the fresh air and the stars overhead. Of course, an apartment was much safer than sleeping outside. Come to think of it, we were pretty lucky during all of that time. We were lucky that nothing bad happened to us!

We actually spoke to a police officer one night while we were on the beach. He explained to us that we were on the border of Monterey and a city called Seaside. Seaside was the city right outside of the Army base and it is also where a lot of those thug soldiers (which I mentioned earlier) ended up living. The police officer told me that Seaside was a very dangerous place to live and he cautioned us in sleeping on the beach. That was nice of him, but we really had no choice at that point.

Frankly I would rather live in poverty on the beach than tell everyone that I had failed and go back to Minnesota to live. No, I was bound and determined to get this right. Besides, California felt more like home to me than Minnesota.

Chapter Twenty

Fighting

Play List
 Kung Fu Fighting
 Carl Douglas
 Ticket to Ride
 The Beatles
 Like a Rollin' Stone
 Bob Dylan

I had been in my fair share of fights growing up. But not too many. I realize that some people go their whole life with out a single fight. But it was not the case when I was growing up. I don't remember ever getting in trouble for fighting, it was just something people did, and often.

And I would like to point out that I never liked fighting. I could handle myself pretty well, but I never liked it.

My older brother for instance was fighting all the time it seemed, and from a very young age. And he said he loved fighting. His second grade report card stated "George is very quick to put up his dukes". I don't remember my father condoning this, but it was not discouraged either. Fighting continued through our school years and unlike today, there was never a punishment for it. But again, he loved it. He told me once that he loved the sound when he punched a guy in the face. To each his own.

I do remember, when I was about ten or so, I was riding on the back of my father's motorcycle in downtown Minneapolis. We had parked in an area that you have to pay to park in. But we did not take up a parking space. That is one thing about a motorcycle, you can usually find a place to park easily. My dad parked his motorcycle inside the paid parking area, but he parked in a grassy area and did not take up a parking space. We finished our business and my dad pulled the motorcycle out and started it. I got on the back of the motorcycle as usual, but when I looked up there was a man standing in front of the motorcycle.

We were about to drive off, but all of a sudden here is this man, and he was not a small man either.

He had his hand on the headlight of my dad's motorcycle and he said, "You need to pay for parking."

Now, I don't really know if my dad would have paid for parking, but there was one problem. This man had his hand on the headlight of my dad's motorcycle. I am not sure what motorcycle etiquette you grew up with, but that was a big no no.

"Get your hand off my bike." That was my dad's response.

Again, if the man had taken his hand off of the motorcycle, I am not sure how this would have played out. Maybe, just maybe, (doubtfully) my dad may have paid for the parking. But that wasn't the case. His hand was on the headlight of my dad's motorcycle.

"You need to pay for parking."

"I said, get your hand off my bike."

"You need to pay for parking."

At this point my dad put the motorcycle on it's kickstand. The motorcycle was still running. I saw my dad reach for his pocket, So I figured this was over. My dad would pay and we would be on our way.

I learned that reaching for your pocket was just a way to catch someone off guard. Because as fast as I saw him reach for his pocket, that same hand shot forward and popped this guy in his nose!

The man fell back on the ground and my dad put up the kickstand and was about to drive off. But now the man was back only now his black eyes were beginning to show and his swollen nose was bleeding profusely. But this parking attendant was one determined individual. He wasn't dumb enough to touch the motorcycle again, but he was in front of the motorcycle once again.

"You need to pay for parking." He was saying it again, but now it was more muffled because of the nose injury. My dad once again put the motorcycle on its kickstand and proceeded to punch and kick this guy as the man back tracked trying to get away from him. The whole time I was sitting on a running motorcycle watching the whole thing!

The parking attendant was now about fifty feet away and laying on the ground, my dad walked back and got on the motorcycle and we started to leave.

One thing you should know about my dad's motorcycle. Most of the time, it had a very tall sissy bar on it. It was for the comfort of the passenger and also came in hand for tying down things when traveling. But as we left, the parking attendant got a hold of this sissy bar and pulled on it. We were riding forward and as he pulled on the sissy bar our front tire went straight up in the air and the motorcycle came crashing down on its side!

I wasn't sure what my dad would do next, now we were both in the gravel of the parking lot and the motorcycle was on its side! I got up as fast as I could, my dad was already to his feet. The parking attendant was no where to be seen, he ran. And it was a good thing he ran, I think my father may have killed him at this point!

My dad started the bike and we were gone. My dad did talk to me about it later, but only to advise me that I may have to go to court.

"Remember, if we go to court, that man tried to hit me first and he called me every name in the book."

We never went to court. But I was now prepared to lie in a court of law.

Chapter Twenty One

A Legal Guardian

Playlist
   Mona
   Bruce Springsteen
   Roll Me Away
   Bob Seger
   People Are Strange
   The Doors

I finally called my dad, but not until we had an apartment and not until I had enrolled in school. I wasn't really sure how to handle that particular situation. Here I was in California and I was living on my own. I thought for sure that the authorities in the school system would need some sort of legal form, proof that I could be in California and proof that I was not a run away. Otherwise I would need to have a legal guardian.

My plan you ask? Well, Tim was twenty-one years of age, he could be a legal guardian! As I said before, I thought for sure that the school authorities would need some sort of legal paperwork. Again, I wasn't sure how to handle that. But the school year was about to start and we had to do something fast. We decided to go to the school, Tim would pose as my legal guardian, and if they needed anything, we would deal with it afterwards.

As it turns out, they didn't require any proof at all. Tim signed all of the paperwork just as any other parent would have. Not once did the legality of his guardianship come up, not once.

I guess the reality of the situation is that not many people are going to lie to the school system to get their kid into school. No one would suspect anything because we were just trying to get me an education.

They were pretty quick about getting my records from my old school in Minnesota. This is where you find out things about other states. The education system in California was a lot more lenient on students than Minnesota. And, I had actually taken a lot of extra classes while I was in high school. I know I said that I was absent from school a lot during high school. But the truth is that high school was very easy for me. I was able to keep above a B average even though I missed a lot of school. Because I had taken so many extra classes, I only had to complete one semester, three months, and I could graduate in California! Can you believe it!

First they accept Tim as my legal guardian. Then they tell me I only need to take a few classes and I could graduate! Things were looking up! We got an apartment, I had a job, and school would be a breeze!

Yes, things were looking up! Unfortunately, Sam proved to be less than reliable. Between showing up with stolen cars and burglarizing nearby businesses, Tim and I actually just wanted Sam to leave. But that did not happen.

When you are a soldier and get arrested, the police do their due diligence and notify the army base. If this happens too often, the army will kick you out of the army. And this is exactly what happened to Sam. Apparently he had broken into a car lot to steal another car. As he was entering through the window (which he had broken) he slipped and cut his leg open. The police heard him screaming for help! Sam claimed that he caught someone breaking into the car lot and this imaginary suspect cut him with a piece of glass. The police didn't buy it and Sam was arrested, of course, after he received medical treatment.

Once he was released from the army, his thieving antics continued. The last time was when he broke into a produce company and stole a produce truck. He was drunk of course. He drove the produce truck through a red light and broadsided another vehicle! He got out of the produce truck and ran. That may have been the end of it, but some everyday heroes saw Sam run away and chased him down and held him for police!

That was the last we saw of Sam. In the meantime I had painted and rebuilt my motorcycle in the living room, well the one room, of our apartment. And yes, it was the same room in which we slept.

During this time Tim was able to get a job working for Wendy's. I was working two jobs (I had quit Joanie's too and found other work that paid better) and one of these jobs was at a steak house. The steak house was a franchise chain and soon I was offered a job as an assistant manager.

This new job offer was hours away in a city near San Francisco. This left me with a dilemma. I wasn't sure how Tim would handle things if I left him. And it seemed unfair that both of us had come to California together and now I was going to leave him alone.

Things have a way of working themselves out and this situation worked itself out as well. Tim met a girl while he was working at Wendy's! It was his second girlfriend in his entire life! And his second time having sex! And now, she was pregnant! What luck! I mean really, what luck! Who has sex one time and gets a venereal disease and the second time he gets a girl pregnant? Tim does just that.

So yes, it worked itself out. Tim went to live with his soon to be wife (yes they got married) and I went to my job in San Francisco.

Epilogue

That was so many years ago. My friend still lives in Monterey with his children and his wife. I on the other hand, well I am still searching for that comfortable place in the sand.

As with all of us, The Movie Never Ends. My movie continues to play as does yours.

Copyright 2024 All Rights reserved

To the Reader:

This is my first Young Adult Novel, and quite frankly probably my last. Horror is m true passion. But somehow, in the midst of my horror novels this book was crying to get out. I hope your movie is an adventure, because like life, The Movie Never ends.

MT Hart is the author of The Mortal Series and much more!

An Awakening in The Mortal Series (4 books in 1)

A Deadly Game in The Formal

A Ghost and a vampire in Casino Agua Caliente

A Puzzling Library in The Wandering Wish

¡Y ahora 4 libros disponibles en español!

PLUS

3 Anthologies